# MALU'S WOLF

## BY RUTH CRAIG

Orchard Books
New York

*For Jack*

Copyright © 1995 by Ruth Craig

All rights reserved. No part of this book may be reproduced or transmitted in any form or by any means, electronic or mechanical, including photocopying, recording, or by any information storage or retrieval system, without permission in writing from the Publisher.

Orchard Books
95 Madison Avenue
New York, NY 10016

Manufactured in the United States of America
Book design by Chris Hammill Paul
10 9 8 7 6 5 4 3 2 1
The text of this book is set in 13 point Weiss.

Library of Congress Cataloging-in-Publication Data

Craig, Ruth.
    Malu's wolf / Ruth Craig.
        p.    cm.
    "A Melanie Kroupa book"—Half t.p.
    Summary: Malu is permitted to raise a wolf cub which eventually is instrumental in bringing about significant changes to the lives and traditions of the young girl's Stone Age clan.
    ISBN 0-531-09484-7. — ISBN 0-531-08784-0 (lib. bdg.)
    [1. Stone age—Fiction.   2. Man, Prehistoric—Fiction.
3. Wolves—Fiction.]    I. Title.
PZ7.C84435Mal   1995
[Fic]—dc20                                    95-6031

# P R E F A C E

Somewhere in Europe, during the Stone Age, lived a girl like Malu. Her people, the Cro-Magnons, were like us—curious, yearning, and resourceful. We have reaped the fruits of their insights and labors, and of those people who lived in the twenty thousand years since. Malu's era was the beginning of it all.

Malu is our ancestor. Kono, the wolf, is the ancestor of all the dogs we have loved. I tell their story so that we will care about these people. Because they endured, we are here.

# CHAPTER ONE

M alu leaped down the hillside path, swinging her sack. Were the wolves back today? For two mornings they'd been gone.

Where the wide path branched, she took the smaller path leading to a rise that overlooked the hollow—the clan's trash hole. Of all the chores assigned to girls, taking the trash down to throw away was the lowliest. But because of the wolves, Malu always chose it.

At the lookout, Malu dropped the sack and scanned the ground beyond the hollow. Ho-la! The wolves *were* back, lying among the spiky tufts of frozen brush. They barely glanced at her, except for the huge black wolf, who stared. Black Chief, Malu called him, for he was the pack's leader.

Malu squinted into the sun, identifying the wolves sprawled around Black Chief. Where was Old Wolf? Malu worried about her, for she often limped behind the pack as they returned from a hunt. Suddenly Old Wolf's tan coat took shape against the brush as she moved to scratch an ear. Malu breathed a sigh of relief.

As Black Chief sat up and yawned, his long red tongue hung out between shiny white fangs. His yellow eyes stared at her. Malu knew better than to look into them, but today she was careless. One glance, and she was locked into his gaze—two blazing suns circled around two black holes drawing her in. It was like sinking into the black holes, down, down—

She blinked her eyes shut, barely in time to break the spell. As everyone knew, you must not look too long into an animal's eyes, for then it could command you to make a vow that you must obey. The hunters never looked into the eyes of animals they were spearing.

When she opened her eyes, Black Chief was looking off to the hills. She had been lucky.

Malu upended the sack and poked through the trash. A broken clay bowl, a shattered flint blade, a broken ax handle, and more. The worst part was the clumps of dried moss clotted with messes—soil from the clan's babies, women's blood, and rotted food. She kicked them down into the hole, holding back the bones to toss to the wolves.

Surprise! Among the boiled-out bones she spied two gristly ones strung with tendons and shreds of meat that would have made rich broth. Someone had been careless. She set them aside.

One by one she flung bones at the wolves. Their eyes tracked them through the air to where they fell. The nestled pair of sand-colored wolves, one with brown ears and the other with a red-tinged head, picked up the two nearest bones and lay down to gnaw. The sleek tan-and-black wolf nudged a small bone and carried it back to his resting spot.

Then the white wolf darted out and snatched a big bone that had fallen near Black Chief. Black Chief stood up majestically, his tail arched high over his back, and stared at the white wolf. Instantly she dropped the bone, tucked her tail under her belly, and slunk away.

Gray Wolf, who'd been watching, rose to stand beside Black Chief, her tail held high like his. She was his mate, the only wolf in the pack who bore cubs. She nosed Black Chief's muzzle, and took the big bone. Black Chief walked over to another bone, and the pair lay down near each other, gnawing companionably.

Was Gray Wolf's belly getting fat? It was too early to be sure. Malu hoped little wolves were growing inside Gray Wolf, like last spring. She had become *very* fat, and two rows of teats swung from her belly when she walked. One day she'd disappeared, and stayed out of sight for many days.

Then one morning, while Malu was watching, Gray Wolf had crawled out from a hole between some rocks. Behind her was a bouncing bundle of fur—no, it was two, three, how many more?—a wild tumble of little black noses, flopped-over ears, wobbly legs, and pointed tails whipping the air.

The big wolves had sprung to their feet. First Black Chief pushed each cub to the ground and sniffed its little upturned belly. Then they all raced about in a frenzy of play.

Gray Wolf had stood apart, watching intently as the other wolves leaped and sidestepped and sprang into the air on stiff legs, like grasshoppers. They slammed their bodies against one another and chased around in wild circles. The babies ran, frisking and wiggling, stumbling and rolling and bouncing. Malu clapped her hands in delight.

She had watched enviously—oh, to share that! She loved them. She loved their joy. If she could run down there, play with them on her hands and knees—be one of them!

Gradually the little wolves lost their dark baby fur and took on their distinctive colors. But as they grew and began to explore, all was not well. In the distance, one day, Malu had seen an eagle fly off with a cub in its talons. Soon another cub was gone. Later, she saw a cub lying listlessly, and by day's end circling vultures soared down to devour it. Only two babies survived, the sand-colored pair Malu saw now, so strong and powerful, chomping on their bones.

Malu sighed, remembering the joy and sorrow. Since then she had watched the wolf pack more and more— from a distance. The wolves never let her get close, though she had tried enticing them by throwing bones halfway up to the lookout point. They always left them lying there until she had gone.

She was their friend, but they didn't seem to know it or even care. She might as well leave now. Reaching for the empty sack, she saw the two meaty bones she had set aside.

Ho-la! Since the wolves wouldn't come to her, maybe *she* could carry the bones to *them*.

Yes! A bone in each hand, she inched down the steep bank. Wolf eyes flicked and wolf ears twitched. When she reached the hollow, they stood up and moved ever so slowly behind Black Chief.

Malu called in the high voice she used with babies, "Here, wolves. Bones with meat and marrow!" She fanned them in the air for them to smell and see.

Black Chief stood motionless, and the others watched, their eyes glittering.

Was this too much of a surprise? Malu trembled. She must be bold—but not too bold. Still waving the bones, she took another step.

Black Chief's eyes narrowed to a slit. What did that mean? Malu gulped and stepped forward again.

Black Chief lowered his head, thrusting it forward, his eyes glinting. Was this a threat? What would he do if she moved closer? She had to find out.

"Bones! Bones!" she sang out softly, and took one more step.

Black Chief wrinkled his snout and bared his fangs. He *was* going to attack! Malu stood frozen.

A long, deep growl rumbled in the air. Malu understood.

*If you give us your leavings, we may accept them. If you keep your distance, we may not attack. Expect no more!*

The bones fell from her fingers. She walked slowly backward toward the hollow, then turned to climb the mound to the lookout.

Picking up her sack, she looked back at the wolves. The bones lay untouched. And Black Chief was still gazing at her.

Malu trudged up the winding hillside path toward the caves. *Expect no more!*

The wolves would never be her friends. But she loved the wolves! What could she do? She walked faster. Somehow, someday, she must find the answer.

# CHAPTER TWO

An icy wind sucked the breath out of Malu when she stepped out of the family cave the next day. She pulled her hood closer about her face as she walked along the ledge, hugging the steep wall of the cliff, passing other small caves with their door skins pulled tight against the cold. The days were getting longer, but spring felt far away.

The Great Ledge in front of the Clan Hall was deserted. On clear days the pale stone cliff was warmed by the winter sun, and children ran and played here, watched over by Malu and the other older girls. But on a day like today everyone would be clustered around the big circular hearth in the Clan Hall, the huge cavern that opened onto the ledge.

Shouts rang out from boys bursting out of the Hall, clutching their slingshots as they raced toward the hillside path, vying to be the first to reach the practice field. Behind them walked the young hunters with their spear-throwers and spears. Some had been initiated into the hunting band, like Malu's cousin Zarbo, while others were still apprentices.

"My spear will fly the farthest!"

Gunto, an apprentice hunter, was boasting again. He'd even said *he* could find the mammoths' new feeding grounds. Never mind that the hunters had spent all winter searching for them! Tomorrow he would go on his Hunt of Passage. If he returned safely, bearing his Tribute, he would take his vows as a member of the hunting band, and become a man.

"Malu," said Zarbo, walking toward her, "you're not feeding the wolves today?"

She held out her slingshot. "I'm going to hunt for birds." As Zarbo lingered, she told him what she'd done yesterday.

He stared at her. "What a terrible risk you took!"

"But nothing happened."

"You were lucky this time. Don't try it again!"

"I won't, *if*"—she laughed—"I can use your spear-thrower!"

He looked around. "Someone might hear you." His voice softened. "I'm sorry you're not a boy." He ran to join the others.

"Taboos!" she muttered. The puny hunting gear of little boys—slingshot and stones—was all that girls and women were allowed to hunt with. At first it had been exciting to learn how to sling stones, to bring down a marmot with one stone, or shoot down a small bird in flight. But she had quickly mastered all a slingshot could do.

The next step—for boys—was the spear-thrower. She ached to try it. How powerfully it sent a spear soaring, to strike down a deer, a boar, a horse—*big game!* Not just little birds and squirrels, mere mouthfuls of meat.

Of all the hunters in the clan, Zarbo was the only one she dared ask about throwing spear. He was closer to her than a cousin—more like a brother, especially since last year, when both his sister and her baby brother had died of the coughing sickness.

\*   \*   \*

The clan bade farewell to Gunto the next day, gathering around the hearth in the Clan Hall. Smoke from the fire wafted up to the high vaulted ceiling, only to disappear into the darkness. He stood, bulky in his leather shirt and pants with the fur side in, and his knee-high boots. Strapped to his back were all his possessions—the rolled-up bearskin for sleeping, his hunting gear, and small sacks of tools, dried moss and tinder, and his fire-making stick.

Gunto bowed his head solemnly as Sosho, the clan's wise man, prayed to the Animal Master, asking him to favor this apprentice hunter. To Malu, Sosho was transformed from her grandfather when he talked to the gods. The heat of the fire made his thin white beard float about his face like a wispy cloud, and as he said the final words to Gunto, his eyes were like blue ice.

Gunto strode out of the Clan Hall, down toward the river valley, to wander alone until he completed his Hunt of Passage. He might be gone a few days or many—however long it took to kill a big animal and bring back all he could carry as his Tribute, a feast for the clan.

The hunters left soon afterward, but went up the hillside path and on beyond the practice field, heading for the mountains. If they were agile and fast enough to track mountain goats, the Animal Master might grant them a few.

In this most harsh of winters, even small game was vital for the clan, and like Malu, many girls and women had taken to hunting. Today Malu rushed down the hillside path into the valley where the trees thinned out. She spotted a snowbird pecking at a bush and killed it with one stone from her slingshot.

When the sun hung low in the west, three small carcasses, the bird and two squirrels, hung from her waist thong as she walked home. Not much meat— but something to add to the goats and the occasional boar that the hunters speared.

\* \* \*

10

That night the moon was round and bright, and from her sleeping shelf Malu heard the wolves howling back and forth to one another, gathering to go on a moonlight hunt.

They usually returned with the rising sun, but at the lookout in the morning, Malu saw that the pack was still away. She shook out her sack and started kicking the trash down the mound.

Then she froze as she heard a furtive scritch-scratching from below. A strange wolf—a lone, scrawny wolf!—was pawing at scraps in the half-frozen pile. Its matted gray-brown coat was slack, but as it moved, Malu could see the fur stretched tight across its swollen belly. A she-wolf—and her birthing time was near!

The wolf's eyes flicked back and forth, but nothing stopped her frantic eating—not the sight of Malu, nor the heavy scent of the wolf pack in the hollow. She was too hungry.

But Malu feared for her, remembering a pack of wolves the hunters had seen. A stray wolf had been lurking about, creeping toward the pack, until the leader chased it off with snarls and snapping jaws. When the stray had slunk back again, the pack surrounded it and killed it.

Black Chief would not tolerate a strange wolf here, she felt, looking across the valley. No wolf pack yet. If only this wolf would go away before it was too late.

"You, Lone Wolf!" she shouted, flapping the air with the empty sack. "Stop eating! Get off with you!"

Lone Wolf kept nosing through the scraps. Malu must chase the wolf away. She took a step down the mound.

But Lone Wolf suddenly stared toward the valley, tucked her tail under her belly, and with a bone in her mouth, bolted up the hill into the trees.

The wolves were coming. They loped lazily toward the mound, looking fat and gorged. They lay down and rolled onto their sides or backs, belly up. They wouldn't stir until tomorrow, she knew, and by then Lone Wolf's scent would be old.

Malu left, worried about Lone Wolf's cubs. A picture from last spring flashed into her mind. What care the pack had lavished on their furry little cubs! How could this poor wolf keep her cubs alive?

She must save them. Find Lone Wolf and bring food to her.

Leaving the path, she tore through brambles and vines, slipping on icy rotted leaves. She peered around boulders, into hollows, under branches, looking for paw prints or scat. Nothing! It would be futile to search through these vast woods.

As she turned back toward home, her foot skidded out from under her, and she fell. Her hand landed on something as hard as stone, but shaped like a stick. She held it up. An antler! An arching piece of antler as long as her forearm.

She traced her fingers along its graceful curves, and

slid her thumb into the smooth groin, where two smaller prongs branched off. The size of it, the form of it! She saw in it a wolf with its head raised to howl. The wolf shape was waiting to emerge from this antler, and with but little carving, it would become a spear-thrower of great beauty.

"I will shape it into the wolf it is meant to be," she told herself. "It will be *like* a spear-thrower, even if it can't *be* one." She tucked it into her waist thong and started running toward home.

But why *not* a spear-thrower? She had found it—or had it found her? It was destined to be hers.

\* \* \*

"It *does* look like a wolf." Varda smiled as she turned it over in her hands.

Malu nodded, glad she had met Varda on the ledge. She rarely saw her anymore, since Varda had become a woman and sat on the women's log benches in the Clan Hall. Before, she and Varda had done many things together. Last spring they were the first girls to bathe in the river after the thaw. Fidday and Talva were good friends, too, but they wouldn't bathe in the icy water, and they'd been afraid to go along when she and Varda made their secret search for the Magic Chamber.

Malu now held up the antler and looked at Varda. "Doesn't it look like—like a spear-thrower?"

"It *looks* like one, but of course . . ." Varda shrugged.

Malu nodded and returned it to her waist thong. This she couldn't tell anyone, not even Varda.

*   *   *

After half a moon Gunto returned from his Hunt of Passage, bending under his burden—his Tribute, the flesh of an elk he had killed. While the women prepared for the feast, he strutted behind the hunting band as they left for his initiation in the Magic Chamber.

Malu watched the procession from the Clan Hall into the passageway that led far into the mountain. They disappeared around the bend, where many smaller tunnels branched off, and then branched off again into even more winding tunnels. Only the hunters knew the way.

Malu and Varda had ventured through some of these tunnels. They only wanted to see where the Magic Chamber was—not to enter it, for to do so would arouse the fury of the gods. Holding torches, lighting one from another as each burned out, they'd followed many twistings and turnings, shuddering at the shadows where the torch suddenly lit up strange rock formations—white towering peaks and shimmering icicles of wet stone.

They'd spoken softly, their voices echoing back as eerie whispers. They'd heard water gurgling somewhere, and mysterious twittering and scratching sounds.

Then the echo of their footsteps had suddenly sounded different. Malu stopped and clutched Varda's arm, and when she lowered her torch to look down, there was nothing but impenetrable darkness below. They stood at the edge of a precipice.

They had turned and fled—come to a dead end—turned back again. A wrong turn into another dead end! Would they ever get out? At last they'd stumbled into the main passageway. They'd run to the Clan Hall, but forced themselves to walk slowly inside. No one but Fidday and Talva had noticed them leave or return.

"You didn't find it?" Fidday had whispered.

Malu had shaken her head, while Varda said, "And we never will."

\*    \*    \*

The aroma of roasting elk meat made Malu breathe deep as she sat with the other girls turning the spits. With her thoughts on her search with Varda, she didn't hear what they were saying until Talva mentioned Gunto.

"Does Gunto really throw spear better than the other hunters?"

Fidday laughed. "His words fly higher than his spear,

I heard. Maybe he didn't kill the elk—just found a dead one!"

Malu said nothing, for she knew more than she should. To see how boys learned to use a spear-thrower, she often hid in the bushes around the practice field. When Gunto's spear flew across the practice field and struck the farthest log, he shouted for everyone to look, and grinned triumphantly.

But he sometimes threw hastily. Once when his spear landed flat on the ground nearby, he banged his spear-thrower on a rock until it split in two—as if the flaw were in it, not himself.

Yet he was being initiated in the Magic Chamber. Any moment, he'd be coming into the Clan Hall.

"Ho-la! Ho-la!" The chanting echoed from the passageway, and the hunting band marched in, led by Sosho and another white-beard, Ullas, the clan's image-maker. He was so old that deep wrinkles puckered his face. Sosho carried aloft the burin, the ancient carved stick of the wise man.

It was Ullas's pictures on the wall of the Magic Chamber that helped the clan keep in the good graces of the Animal Master. Woe be to any clan that lacked an image-maker like Ullas! For the fickle Animal Master was easily offended and could withhold game from the hunters.

The two elders stopped at the hearth and turned to face the clan. The hunters, their spears pointed up, formed a half-circle, with the rest of the clan gathered behind. Sosho waved the burin, and Gunto stepped forward.

Malu inched her way around the crowd to see. Gunto's left hand, covered with red paint, was pressed to his chest. She even saw paint spatters on his wrist. She couldn't stop looking at it. Why red paint on a new hunter's hand? So many mysteries. "Taboo!" she muttered, as if it were a curse.

Sosho spoke of the Hunt of Passage. "When Gunto saw the elk, he killed it with respect, and brought its flesh as his Tribute. Behold his red hand, the sign that he is bound by the hunters' vows. The paint will fade, but the honor will remain. All hail to Gunto!"

"Gunto, the hunter!" the clan called out three times. But the clan's voices were dutiful, not like the hearty shouts last year when Zarbo was hailed.

Sosho waved the burin, ending the ceremony. Varda and the other younger women began setting out the feast on the broad benches by the hearth. When Malu and the other girls took the meat off the spits, their share of the work was over.

Malu walked restlessly around the Clan Hall, behind the clusters of people talking. She was thinking again about the mystery of the red hand. If only—

A burst of laughter stopped her. She'd nearly walked into the small circle of hunters around Gunto. Jesting with the newly initiated hunter, though not part of the initiation, was a tradition for the younger hunters. The taunts were their way of acknowledging that the initiate was one of them. After each hunter's taunt, the initiate would answer with a jest of his own, the wittier the better.

Malu didn't hear the jest, or who had made it. The laughing died as the hunters looked expectantly at Gunto. Instead of a smiling answer, Gunto turned red and snarled words Malu couldn't hear.

Knowing she shouldn't witness the jesting, she started inching backward to avoid being noticed. Then she heard Zarbo's voice, strong and clear. She stood still. She just had to hear Zarbo's jest.

"I thought we'd be feasting on mammoth tonight, Gunto, but that roasting meat smells a lot like elk to me!"

The hunters whooped and roared, and again looked to Gunto.

Gunto bared his teeth like an animal and jabbed his spear at Zarbo's chest, the point nicking his leather shirt.

Zarbo, standing stone-still, curled his lip and stared back.

No one moved. Then one of the hunters pushed aside Gunto's spear. "Stay, Gunto," he said softly. "The answer to a jest is another jest."

"Ha!" Gunto snorted. "Hear *my* jest. Next time, Zarbo, my spear won't stop at your shirt." He pushed his way through the circle.

"Shame, Gunto!" one of the youths called out after him. The hunters exchanged glances, but said no more.

Malu realized Gunto was coming her way. She pressed herself against the wall, but it was too late. He stopped, glared, and spat on the wall close to her head, before striding on by.

By now the hunters had wandered off toward the hearth, but Zarbo came to Malu.

"What did Gunto do?" he said through pinched lips. She told him.

"Our new hunter! Watch out for him, Malu."

Malu nodded, and went to sit with the other girls for the feast. They had seen nothing, and Malu didn't speak of it. She sat staring into the fire, knowing Gunto wouldn't forget that she had seen him shamed—she, of all people, Zarbo's cousin and a *girl*.

*   *   *

*Ma-luuuuu!*

Malu sat up in her sleeping shelf. The wolves often howled at the time of the full moon. But tonight they called her name! *Come, Malu. Hear us, Malu.*

She tiptoed to the entrance, careful not to disturb the slow rhythm of her parents' sleeping breaths. Tumbling clouds swept across the sky, and through them the moon glowed, cold and serene. She had never seen the Moon Goddess look so full and powerful.

Now many wolf voices, near and far, joined the eerie song, rising and falling, weaving its strands about her as she swayed back and forth. Moon-wolf, wolf-moon.

They were one, and the goddess spoke to her through wolf voices.

*You have honored my kin, the Clan of Wolves. You cannot save Lone Wolf, but soon one of her cubs will need you.*

"The woodland is so vast! Where can I find Lone Wolf and her cubs?" Malu whispered.

*You cannot find them. You will come upon them . . . come upon them . . . come . . .*

Clouds roiled across the moon. The voices dwindled to a lone sinking howl. Shivering, she waited, but there was only silence and blackness. She ran across the cold rock floor to her sleeping shelf.

*       *       *

The next day she sat on a boulder near the lookout, recalling the Moon Goddess's words as she polished the wolf that had emerged from her antler. She blew the last bit of pumice dust from it. It was finished. She caressed the wolf it had become, and knew it was a worthy spear-thrower.

All that remained was to *use* it—throw a spear with it. She had no spear, of course. She would have to think about that.

As she walked home, the Moon Goddess's message drummed in her mind. *You will come upon them. You will come upon them.* Lone Wolf and the cubs were somewhere, and that was all she could know—until when?

*  *  *

Holding her spear-thrower under her shirt, she sat hidden in the underbrush as some boys took their first instruction from Zarbo. One boy stood with his right hand palm up by his shoulder, holding a spear-thrower.

"Like this," Zarbo said, pushing the boy's thumb and fingers together to circle around the spear-thrower.

Then he pried the boy's fingers open just enough to slide the blunt end of a spear along the top of the thrower. The hook at the end of the thrower was facing forward, to meet the hole at the end of the spear. She heard a faint click as they slipped together.

"Keep the spear pointed forward and up—balance it with your left hand until you lunge." The boy nodded. "Now—lunge!"

The spear flew up but landed close by. The boy grimaced, but Zarbo called it a fine first throw.

When the next boy lunged, the spear-thrower flew out of his hand with the spear.

"That's the hard part," said Zarbo, "keeping your fingers tight on the thrower but loose on the spear."

Malu watched intently, moving her fingers and arms the way he showed the boys.

Finally everyone left. She found a long, fairly straight stick and gouged out a hole in the end with the small knife she always carried. With her spear-thrower and improvised spear, she lunged into her first throw. The stick flew up, but waggled and fell. She had to do better than that! She threw again.

"What are you *doing*!"

Zarbo's voice. She whirled around. He had returned! He and Ardap, his adopted younger brother, stood there, mouths agape.

"You—you—" Zarbo choked. "Let me see what you're throwing with. Not that stick—the spear-thrower!"

She handed it to him. He looked it over. "A wolf. Good shape. Where did you get it?"

She found her voice, and told him of the antler, and of seeing the wolf in it—and even of spying on them to see how to throw.

"So," said Zarbo. "That's how bad you want it." His voice sounded approving, but he said, "I'm not going to help you."

"I don't want you to break your vows," she said quickly.

"You threw quite well, with a no-good stick."

Ardap spoke for the first time. "I'm making a longer spear for myself. I'll leave my old one around here somewhere. Maybe you'll find it."

She was astonished. Ardap rarely spoke to her, and now—this.

Zarbo put on an exaggerated frown. "You *children* can do as you please. Don't expect any help from me."

"We know." Ardap flashed Malu a shy smile.

* * *

Malu found the spear hidden behind a rock. She practiced throwing it every day that the hunting band and apprentices were away on a hunt. One day she was throwing so well with Ardap's old spear that she forgot to notice the sun. It still seemed like early morning. As the spear soared almost to the farthest log in the field, she jigged up and down with delight.

"Malu! Hide! The hunters are almost here!" Ardap shouted from the path.

Clutching the spear-thrower, Malu broke into a run and, heading away from the path, crashed through the wild underbrush. Scratches and bruises—nothing mattered but getting far away. Then she'd circle around before turning back home.

She ran until she had to lean against a tree to catch her breath. She was in a dense part of the woods that she'd never seen. Looking around, she picked her way among rocks and fallen branches. A shadow on the ground ahead—there was a movement. She stepped forward, ready to turn and run.

Lone Wolf! The wolf raised her head, staring at Malu. The words of the Moon Goddess drummed in her head. *You will come upon them. . . .*

She bent over Lone Wolf. The stink of death made her cough. Lone Wolf's tongue, thin and shriveled, dangled out of her mouth. The cubs were clustered about her wasted body. Three lay lifeless. One looked up at Malu. That was the one!

Lone Wolf's yellow eyes were sunk deep in their sockets. Even so, they were blazing. Malu looked into them, and felt the wolf's grinding, wasting emptiness inside that no food could fill. The eyes drew her in, and she leaned closer. She *wanted* the vow Lone Wolf would command her to make.

*Vow to care for my cub when I die. Swear to it, Malu, swear by the Moon Goddess!*

"I vow to care for your cub. By the Moon Goddess, I swear it."

Lone Wolf's nose pointed skyward. As she blew out her last breath, her head thumped to the ground.

Malu blinked hard. Lone Wolf was gone. And Lone Wolf's cub was hers! She touched it and shrank back. It had pushed its nose into her hand! She had never touched a living animal—only prey she had killed, and they didn't move.

Her wolf! She cupped her hands around its belly and felt the pulse of life as she set it against her shoulder. The cub snuggled into her neck, its tiny pointed tail whipping lightly across her chin. She squeezed it gently. Its soft, fast breaths warmed her neck. It whimpered.

She *liked* this little wolf! She even liked holding it!

It? She sat down and turned it over. She wasn't sure, but it looked like a she-wolf. She laughed, and the

24

tiny pointed ears twitched. The cub could hear her! It looked at her with dark shining eyes! Did wolf eyes turn yellow later? She touched her fingertip to the fine gray hair of its chest, and a little pink tongue licked her finger.

The cub scratched to get down, swinging its tail in little circles. She smiled, looking at the pointed ears perked over the black head and muzzle. She picked it up again. Under its soft dark fur, the cub was bone-thin. She must take it home and feed it. She walked fast.

Take a wolf home? What would people think? They liked meat, not animals. They killed animals with respect because of the powerful Animal Master—not because they *liked* them.

"Oh, little wolf," she murmured, "what can I do with you?"

She was at the hillside path, where anyone might see them. What if she turned down the path and left the cub at the hollow for the wolf pack to find? They had no cubs now. They might adopt her, like Ardap, when he was little. After the hunters had found him wandering around all alone, Zarbo's parents had made him their second son.

Would the wolves adopt a cub? Or would they snap at her and rip her apart? She could not take that risk.

Would Mother and Father help her? Sosho—what would *he* think?

There was no answer. She stuffed the cub inside her shirt and shook out her long hair to lie across her chest. She ran up to the ledge, with a smile for the people sitting there, and ran on.

"Where have you been for so long?" said Mother, turning from the small hearth as she stirred the embers with a stick.

"I was—walking," she said. She felt the cub moving around inside her shirt. The tiny claws were scratching her skin, and she couldn't help but wriggle.

"Have you got something under your shirt, Malu?"

The cub was crawling up her chest and whining a tiny whine. Mother's eyes opened wide.

Malu groped for the cub and set her on the floor.

Mother drew back with a gasp. "What is it? Where did you get that—that *animal?*"

"Malu!" Father's voice boomed at her from the entrance. She turned and saw his face white with shock.

She held the wolf cub close as Father strode in, glaring at her. She looked from Father to Mother, trying to put her longing into her eyes so that they'd understand.

"It's only a wolf cub—an orphan. I have to keep her alive."

"You certainly don't have to!" Father said. "Whatever made you think that?"

"Because . . . ," Malu said. Without mentioning the practice field, she told about the Moon Goddess's message and coming upon Lone Wolf in the woods. Then she came to the worst part.

"Father, Mother, I—I made a vow. I swore by the Moon Goddess to keep this cub alive."

"You swore by the Moon Goddess!" Father whispered.

"I did wrong, to look into Lone Wolf's eyes, and then I had to say yes and swear."

Father grimly shook his head. "I have to tell Sosho. The hunters must meet in the Magic Chamber."

He paused at the entrance. "What a rash child you are! Didn't you think about the Animal Master? He might turn his wrath on us—take away our hunting magic. We could all starve!"

"I'm sorry, Father!" Tears wet her eyes. He was gone.

"Malu, my daughter," Mother said, "where do your strange ideas come from? What will happen to you?"

She couldn't answer. The cub whimpered and chewed her finger.

# CHAPTER THREE

Mother shook her head. "That little animal needs food. I can't see it being hungry." Taking dried meat from the keeping shelf, she dropped a piece on the floor.

The cub eagerly mouthed it—and, choking, spit it out.

"Oh, she's sick!" cried Malu. Then she remembered how the wolf pack had fed their cubs after a hunt. They vomited meat onto the ground, which the little cubs eagerly devoured.

This cub just couldn't chew meat yet. But Malu could. She chewed a piece into a slimy lump and spit it on the floor.

The cub sniffed and, with a tiny yelp, ate it and licked the spot on the floor. Malu chewed and spat until the cub stopped eating. When she picked her up, the little belly was round and solid.

"Mother! Someday, I know this little wolf will reward you. She will!"

"Who knows what lies ahead?" Mother said. "I must go to the Clan Hall. Wait here with the cub until the hunters return from the Magic Chamber and tell you what to do."

The cub slept. Malu waited. At last footsteps stopped outside the family cave, and Sosho entered without speaking. The cub woke up. Sosho looked long at her. Suddenly the cub squatted, making a puddle at his feet. Malu closed her eyes. What a time for the cub to do this!

"Malu," said Sosho, "take the wolf cub to the Clan Hall." He swept out of the cave.

After soaking up the puddle with dried moss, Malu went out, carrying the cub in her arms. She trembled when she saw people standing on the Great Ledge, looking at her, scowling and frowning. Many drew near for a closer look, exchanging glances of disbelief. She walked faster.

"Animal!" someone muttered.

"A wolf! How could she!" A young mother held tight to her small daughter's hand.

Malu couldn't keep silent. "It's only a *baby*, an orphan. She won't bother anyone."

"Little wolves grow into big wolves," said the woman, "and big wolves kill!"

Gunto held up his spear. "I know what to do with wolves!"

Malu rushed into the Clan Hall. Sosho beckoned her to the hearth. People were gathered before him, their eyes fixed on her and the wolf cub. She saw Mother's face, and her tiny nod that said *Be brave.* She breathed deep and stood taller.

"Behold Malu's wolf," Sosho said. "The Moon Goddess has decreed that the wolf cub will live with our clan."

The cub could stay! This was more than she'd dared to hope. But she heard gasps of surprise and fear. She looked down at the furry little cub and held her closer.

"Hear me." Sosho raised his hand. He told of the Moon Goddess speaking to Malu in the voices of wolves. "As foretold, Malu came upon the one surviving cub, and made a vow to the Moon Goddess: to care for the cub."

He looked around at the clan, nodding, his eyes resting on many of their faces. "The wolf cub will live with us under Malu's care."

He had said it! She shut her eyes to hide her joy, lest it appear unseemly. There was an undercurrent of voices, and Sosho asked if anyone wanted to speak. That was his way.

"The wolf will grow big and attack us!"

"I understand your fear," Sosho said. "Now hear this, also: If the wolf ever harms one of the people, the Moon Goddess decrees that the wolf must be killed."

Malu looked up at Sosho. His eyes glittered. He was the clan's wise man now, not her grandfather. She bowed her head. Her wish had been granted. Yes, but what a heavy weight—whether the cub lived or died depended on her.

She looked down at the cub in her arms—little nose of moist black leather, perked ears, dark eyes shining at her. The cub pawed at her shoulder and nestled into her neck. Her wolf!

A fierceness swelled within her. She would let nothing happen to this baby wolf. She heard another question asked.

"Isn't it taboo for animals to live with people?"

Sosho shook his head. "Animals haven't lived with people before, but it is not taboo."

"But keeping the wolf here, won't it offend the Animal Master?" said a young hunter.

"I was about to speak of that," Sosho said. "The Animal Master's law is that animals must live with respect for each other. They must not kill others wantonly, or for bloodlust. They may kill only for food or for self-defense. If wolves and people live together within this law, the Animal Master is content." He nodded. "The wolf can stay with us. So be it."

People exchanged glances. Off to the side, Gunto scowled fiercely. Of those leaving the Clan Hall, many looked doubtful, and some cast indignant looks her way. Curious and smiling, Malu's friends came for a closer look at the wolf cub—Fidday and Talva, Zarbo and Ardap, Varda and others.

Fidday patted the cub's head. "She's like a baby!"

"I'm glad you have your wolf," said Varda. Malu wanted to talk to her, but others were pushing in to see the cub.

Sosho took Mother, Father, and Malu aside. His first words surprised Malu. "The wolf needs a name. Kono is the name I have chosen, for it is not fitting to give her a people's name."

Kono. She liked the sound of it. She repeated the name to herself and smiled, until she saw Sosho, unsmiling, stare at her. Those icy blue eyes could look into her head where her spirit dwelt.

"Malu, to keep Kono from doing harm is not enough. You must make the clan see Kono as a friend and helper."

"Yes, Sosho. I *want* to! I will, I promise." He turned away, and she carried Kono home.

She fed Kono as before, and played with her, whisking a strip of elk hide along the floor. Kono pounced, grabbed it in her teeth, and braced her paws to tug at it. How strong this little creature was! As Malu laughed, Kono yanked the strip from her fingers and ran outside. Malu caught her and set her down at the back of the cave.

Kono nipped Malu's ankle and ran in circles, dashing again to the doorway. Again Malu caught her. She put Kono on the sleeping shelf. Kono peered over the edge. Malu knew she'd quickly learn to jump off.

Kono whimpered. Malu took her off the shelf, Kono ran, and Malu picked her up at the doorway.

"Is she going to keep running around like that?"

Mother asked. Father looked sharply at Kono but said nothing.

"I'll think of something," Malu said. To distract Kono, she grabbed the piece of hide and shook it. Kono leaped on it and tugged it with her teeth.

A vision came to her. While they were both tugging the piece of hide, it held them together—except that Kono could let go of it. If she could *fasten* it to Kono—! But not this worn-out scrap.

She took a long, sturdy strap from the keeping shelf and made a loop at one end with the slipknot hunters used in trapping. She slid it over Kono's head. Yes! Kono shook her head and looked surprised, but it held.

"Now she can go with me anywhere!" Her parents smiled, and she took Kono out for her first walk.

*　*　*

In the morning she sopped up a puddle on the floor with some dried moss. It looked as if she'd have to make many trips to the storage chamber to get moss. She led Kono down to the pine grove below the cliff, where people went to relieve themselves. Kono sniffed around eagerly, and squatted to make another puddle.

The smells meant something to Kono. Malu let Kono lead her around until Kono left a pile of dung by a pine tree.

"What a smart wolf!" Kono wriggled and licked her hand.

Before taking trash down to the lookout, she took Kono home and tethered her to a rock outcropping. She feared the worst would happen if Kono and the wolf pack ever saw each other.

The wolves sprawled on the ground below the lookout. Black Chief glanced at her and yawned. Gray Wolf sat near him, sniffing at a tuft of dried grass. The others chased one another, leaping over rocks and zigzagging, the chasers suddenly becoming the chased. Suddenly they all lay down, panting, eyes gleaming in the sun.

They seemed to be smiling. Did wolves smile? She was sure they did.

Two wolves started tossing a stick in the air, pretending to fight over it. A third wolf ran at them, and launched itself sideways, giving one of them a powerful body slam. All the others—even Black Chief and Gray Wolf—ran in to join them, and they dashed about in a frenzy of body slamming. They suddenly stopped, howled together, and loped off toward the river.

Wolf play! Poor Kono, a little lone cub tied to a rock. Kono needed wolf play. If not with wolves, maybe with children.

She led Kono to the Great Ledge where the little children played, watched by the older girls. Kono frisked toward Fidday, whipping her tail in an arc.

"Funny little wolf." Fidday knelt and laughed as Kono's nose snuffled noisily against her chin.

"Me! Me!" shouted Talva's little brother Yubar.

Before Malu could pull her back, Kono had licked his face. Yubar's eyes opened wide. Malu held her breath. Was he going to scream? But he laughed and shouted again, "Me! Me!"

*Hoo!* breathed Malu.

The other children, who'd been backing away, rushed in, pushing their faces at Kono to be licked, grabbing her fur, touching her nose, tugging her ears. Greeted with loud giggles and shrieks, Kono dashed among them. What fun they were having together!

Kono bounded around them in exuberant stiff-legged leaps, playfully nipping and pawing. As they screeched, Kono leaped higher and faster.

Kono was becoming so excited that she could accidentally injure a small child. Malu pulled the strap to draw Kono close, and walked her home, with Kono whimpering and pulling toward the children. Malu realized she must keep the play sessions short.

As time went on, Malu thought longingly of her spear-thrower, lying under her sleeping shelf ever since she'd found Kono. Kono was taking much more of her time than Malu had ever expected. But Kono needed her.

\* \* \*

The moon thinned and became round again, two times. Winter was yielding to spring, and the sun warmed the Great Ledge. Under her sleeping shelf one day, Malu came upon a much-chewed strip of elk hide, the very one she and Kono used to play with. Running her fingers over it, she felt something small and hard stuck in it, and plucked it out. A tiny white tooth! Kono's baby tooth? Wolves must have baby teeth, as people did. But look at Kono now, her tongue hanging out between those long, sharp fangs!

"Ho-la! *When* did you grow those, Kono? Remember how I used to chew your meat for you?" She pressed the strip of hide to her cheek, and after poking the tooth back into it, she rolled it up and tucked it into her treasure sack.

Sitting on the floor by Kono, she ran her fingers through her fur, feeling its thickness, almost like the coat of a grown wolf, her tail full and brushy. Her coat color had changed, too. Her tail, back, and top of her head remained black, but her face and the rest of her body were shades of gray, white, and tan. A dash of brown above her eyes—which were now a glowing yellow—gave her a questioning, curious look.

Kono looked up with her black-rimmed eyes, as warm and glowing as twin suns.

"Did Ullas paint those black lines around your eyes, and around your mouth?" she said. "What a pretty wolf you are!"

But this pretty wolf, so much bigger now, was harder to handle than she'd ever dreamed. Her capers and wild play made some people smile, but others shrank back. Malu warned herself: *Always hold the strap tight. Never let Kono take you by surprise.*

One day while walking along the rocky ledge, Kono suddenly gave Malu a body slam that knocked her to her hands and knees. She wasn't hurt—but she was shocked to realize how powerful Kono was. What if Kono body-slammed a young child now?

She mustn't let it happen. She held Kono's strap tight when children were near, and stopped taking her to the ledge for play.

But older boys, who had ignored Kono till now, liked the rough play. When they saw her, they ran and shouted to excite Kono into making body slams at them—laughing when they got knocked down, shouting when they could withstand the slam.

This was good for now, but with Kono growing ever bigger and stronger, Malu knew she'd have to put a stop to this, too. And then what?

\* \* \*

The moon thinned again and once more grew round, and the greening season was upon them. Malu felt most of the clan was accepting Kono. True, some still stepped aside or frowned at the sight of her, but most took little note of the wolf.

Malu still took trash to the lookout, sorting out the choice morsels for the wolf pack. She didn't forget her spear-thrower, either, though it remained unused, under her sleeping shelf. She must start throwing spear again! Soon, she hoped.

As she walked along the ledge with Kono on a clear day, she stopped to look out over the valley. New growth covered it like a green haze, and when she squinted, she thought she could even see the river flowing in the distance. Spring was really here.

*"Hoo!"* Her wrist was burning! The strap—Kono was loose, leaping down the cliff! She *had* let Kono take her by surprise.

"Kono!" she screamed.

Kono skidded farther on down on all four feet.

"Come back!" Malu shouted. But Kono kept going.

The cliff was too steep—but she *must* get Kono. She jumped, falling and rolling, sitting up, sliding—calling Kono over and over. Kono turned her head, but paid no heed.

Then Kono turned back, scratching her way up the pebbly cliff toward Malu. But before she could grab the strap, Kono jumped out of reach and stood panting, eager for more play. Malu shook her head in despair.

Kono climbed higher. The strap was close to Malu's fingertips. She lunged for it.

Too far! She tumbled over and over. Her hand touched a gnarled root, and she hung on. She leaned into the cliff, crying with fear for Kono. She'd never catch her.

A damp nose burrowed into her neck. "Oh, you—

you wolf!" Sobbing, she clutched Kono's ruff and felt for the strap.

After struggling back up the cliff, she sat on a rock, limp, trying to catch her breath. Kono stirred. Malu looked up. Sosho was standing there.

"You saw it all?" she said.

He nodded. "Malu, how does a wolf play with other wolves?"

What a strange question. "A wolf chases around and bites the other wolves' fur and jumps on them and slams his body against them. . . ."

"And Kono, with people?" Sosho raised his eyebrows.

"Kono plays like a wolf. She can hurt people. She's so big and strong, but she's—she doesn't know much about being with people," said Malu in a very little voice.

"Isn't that because you haven't taught her?"

"I—I don't know how to teach her," she whispered. "I thought the strap was enough, but it isn't."

"Then isn't it up to you, Malu, to find a way?" Sosho tapped her lightly on the head and was gone.

Leading Kono home, Malu moaned, "Why can't Sosho tell me what to do—not ask questions that have no answers?"

She asked Mother and Father, "How can I teach her?"

"You know more about wolves than we do," Father said. "It's up to you."

Those same words! It *was* up to her. That night her head was awhirl with ideas, none of them any good. In the morning, with her spear-thrower under her shirt, Malu took Kono up to the practice field. It was desserted, for the hunters had left early to track down goats in the mountains.

She threw the spear, and that was no good, either. She hid it back in the bushes, and sat rubbing her fingers over and around the spear-thrower wolf. It felt warm, even warmer than her fingers—as if it had become alive under her touch.

*To teach a wolf, take a wolf hunting.*

What had put these words in her mind? She looked at the spear-thrower, wondering. It felt hard and cold again.

"Come, Kono!"

She picked up her slingshot and stones and took off with Kono, holding Kono's strap until they had gone far into the woods.

When she slipped the loop off of Kono's head, the wolf looked at her, head cocked. Then like a stone shot from a sling, she dashed out of sight, and bounded back to her with long, powerful leaps. Malu laughed, entranced to see Kono free, frisking around, running back to lick her hand, dashing away again.

Kono slowed down, sniffed and snuffled around bushes, burrowing her nose in the moldy leaves strewn on the ground. What a richness of smells for a wolf.

Looking around, Malu realized she'd been near here

once before. She looked up the hill—yes, this was the place. Kono bounded back to her and stood quietly at her side.

Malu said, "Lone Wolf, here is your cub, Kono. I have kept my vow."

A breeze shook the leaves overhead. Flickers of light and shadow danced around her. She tingled, knowing it was Lone Wolf's spirit stirring the air.

The air was still once more, and she walked on.

"Go, Kono! Find something for me to shoot!"

Kono trotted forward. A bird stood in the path ahead. Kono leaped, wings flashed, and the bird was perched in a tree. Kono looked up, puzzled.

"A bird, Kono. You can't catch birds," said Malu, laughing as she pulled a stone from her sack. "Now stand still."

But Kono leaped against the tree trunk, and the stone struck the empty branch.

"Don't scare away game!" Malu cried out. Would she ever be able to hunt with Kono? Or teach her anything? She put the strap on her again.

They walked on, as the hill leveled out near the valley. At every rustling leaf or snapping twig, Malu tugged Kono to a halt and stood motionless to look around. Kono looked around, too.

Farther on, Kono stood still when Malu could hear nothing at all, and her nose, with eager rapid sniffs, caught scents that Malu would never smell.

Ho-la! With Kono at her side, she could hunt with

a wolf's keen ears and nose! She could bring home more meat. Her empty belly growled.

"Come, Kono! Find something for me!"

They walked along easily as the trees thinned out. Malu held a stone in her sling, on the ready. Suddenly Kono stopped short. Nothing happened. Malu was about to nudge Kono with her toe, but Kono's rigid stance and fixed stare made her wait.

Leaves rustled, and a huge hare hopped into view, nibbling grass. What a splendid hare! And being this close, she couldn't miss. Taking careful aim, she pulled back on the sling.

Kono leaped. The strap burned Malu's wrist. The slingshot fell from her hands. Kono streaked through the grass, the strap flying behind her.

That hare—the first good game she'd seen all day—her meat—it was gone!

"Bad! Bad wolf!" Anger steamed through her. She seized the strap with both hands and gave it a furious yank.

Kono choked and stumbled. She had hurt Kono! She must hug her, comfort her.

But Kono was acting very strange. With her head turned to one side, she flicked the tip of her tongue in and out of her mouth. Her legs folded into a crouch, she crawled on her belly toward Malu.

Like the cubs with Black Chief! He had growled and snapped at them. They crawled to him on their bellies—submitting to Black Chief, their leader.

And now . . . "I am *your* leader," she whispered. She longed to hug Kono, but remembered—Black Chief standing motionless, making the cubs wait.

She stood straight and tall, staring down at Kono. She held out her hand, and Kono licked it.

She waited, staring into Kono's intent yellow eyes.

"Stay there!" she said in her deepest voice. Kono quivered, but did not move.

With another "Stay there!" she stepped back one step, then another. Kono's legs twitched, but she stood still.

*Now* it was time. She stood still. "Come, Kono!"

Kono bounced over to her, tail thumping with the same abandon she'd seen in the cubs greeting Black Chief. She clung to Kono, and as the big pink tongue washed over her chin, she breathed a silent prayer. *Thank you, Moon Goddess, for Kono.*

She had found the answer! What a wolf taught a cub with a growl, a person could do with a commanding voice. She'd never spoken like this before. Anger had taught her how to.

"Kono! My wolf!" She dropped to her knees and grabbed Kono. With Kono yipping and Malu laughing, they tumbled and rolled over and over—two wolves.

Malu, breathless, finally stood up. "Come, Kono. You've got to learn more about hunting. Now!" She didn't have to be angry to sound commanding. Kono stood before her, alert. Again they stalked and listened.

A dove flew off because Kono couldn't stay still long enough. Three times, then, she made Kono practice staying in place as she walked away. Each time she called, Kono rushed at her with bushy tail waving wildly, and each time Malu sang out loud praises.

They started walking again. Kono stopped her. A squirrel sat under a tree ahead. Kono stood quietly—though trembling with excitement—as Malu shot a stone and killed it. Malu cut out the guts for Kono to eat, and hung the little carcass on her waist thong.

Farther on, Kono stopped again. Though Malu saw and heard nothing, she trusted Kono. Another squirrel darted into sight, and another stone took it down. Kono gulped down the guts, and Malu added a second carcass to her waist thong.

She had Kono at her side, Kono's ears and nose—and she was Kono's leader! She wanted to leap and run and flap her arms—but the sun was lowering, and a long walk was ahead. She walked on steadily, side by side with Kono. She felt Kono's teeth touch her fingers, knowing instantly it wasn't a bite. Kono's mouth was holding her hand.

"Kono—my friend," she whispered. Her throat was too tight to give voice. Coming close to home, she felt hope. Knowing what she knew now, she *could* teach Kono to live with people.

Climbing the path, she heard people talking. She looped the strap over Kono's head.

"Stay close to me, Kono." Malu tugged the strap

gently, walking up the hillside path as her wolf bobbed lightly against her leg. The strap hung loose between them, and even when two men carrying fishnets trotted past, Kono only sniffed the air.

Proudly, Malu knew that if Kono understood what her leader wanted, she would do it. She sang out softly, "What a good wolf you are, Kono! I must tell Sosho!"

Coming out of the woods onto the ledge, she blinked at the sun striking the pale rock face of the cliff. People basked in the warmth, even Sosho, who was hardly ever idle. He sat on a rock with eyes half-closed. As Kono's claws clicked on the rock surface, he looked up, his keen eyes going from the strap dangling between her and Kono to the carcasses hung at her waist.

"I think something has changed, Malu."

"Yes, Sosho." Malu drew herself up, trying to act more like the leader she had become. "Kono taught me how to be her leader. She obeys me. And I taught her how to hunt with me."

When he smiled, she couldn't hold back the rush of words. "Oh, Sosho, Kono *is* a helper! She hears animals before I can. She even stopped me when I would have walked ahead and scared them away! That's how I got these." She pointed to her waist.

"Tell me how this came about," Sosho said.

And she did. He listened, asking an occasional question.

"You are fulfilling your vow. I'm proud of you, Granddaughter."

45

He patted her shoulder, touched Kono's head, and walked into the Clan Hall.

"Ho-la!" Malu whispered to herself, though she wanted to shout. Sosho had never spoken to her like this! These were words to bask in, words warmer than the sun. She threw her arms around her wolf. "Kono, he knows how good you are!"

# CHAPTER FOUR

The clan began counting on this spring's running of the deer to the northlands. As they always did, the hunters went to the river when the first deer rushed along the trail across the valley. It was easier to spear them as they slowed down to plunge in the river and swim across.

But the spring running lasted only a day this year. Why, no one knew.

"Animals of the hoofed clans are giddy," said Ullas. "They follow the same trail year after year and then, for no reason, make a new trail."

With deer meat scarce, the hunters ranged farther every day, looking for deer or other big game, but glad to bring home even small game. Malu took Kono hunting, too, and even girls and younger women who seldom hunted set out with slingshots. Though the clan wasn't close to starving, people

were getting thinner and feared they were losing
their strength.

*   *   *

Malu didn't dare let Kono run free. She looked like
a grown wolf but wanted to play like a frisky cub, and
in children she saw creatures of her own kind. When
two little boys chased by, whooping and screeching,
Kono eagerly leaped at them. If Malu hadn't pulled
back on the strap with both hands, she would have
knocked them over.

The days grew longer. Leaf buds plumped and burst
open on trees and bushes. The clan deserted the Clan
Hall these days, making the Great Ledge their work-
place. Women and girls carried out their baskets, bowls,
and animal pelts. Small children ran around in play, while
older ones braided ropes or worked on leather straps.
Hunters honed axes, knives, and spearpoints.

Malu knelt, scraping flesh from the underside of a
hare's pelt, tossing the scrapings to Kono. She laughed
to see those huge jaws, which could break the leg of
a deer, snap shut on the bits of meat, but she saw that
the real fun was catching them.

The girls talked as they worked, wondering when
the clan would leave for the summer huts. The hunting
might be better there, and they'd have the fruits of
the plants and trees, and the roots of the soil.

"Look how thin I am," grumbled Talva, pointing to

her belly. Like the rest of the clan, they worried that they might lose their precious fat, the sign of strength and endurance.

"I didn't know my arms were so bony," said Malu.

"When are we ever going to go!" said Fidday.

* * *

"It is time," Sosho said after two more warm days. "Prepare to leave tomorrow for the summer grounds." When the children shouted joyfully, his smile deepened the creases in his face.

Malu and her parents shoved winter things under their sleeping shelves—their bear-hide sleeping skins and furry winter clothing. They would take with them dried meat to eat on the trek, and everything they needed for the summer. Light deerskin clothing was stuffed into sacks, with clay vessels, a stone lamp, reed baskets, fire sticks, kindling, and dried moss. Deerskin sleeping skins were rolled up and tied. And Father's hunting gear, of course.

Before dawn they shouldered their sacks and went to the Great Ledge. Malu tightened the shoulder thongs that bound her sacks. She had hidden her spear-thrower among her belongings, and Ardap had told her he'd carry her spear along with his new one.

"You're going to like the trek," Malu said, hugging Kono, who sat beside her on the Great Ledge, looking around, eyes sparkling curiously.

Talking and laughing, the clan waited for Sosho. Smaller children stamped around proudly bearing little sacks lashed to their backs. Only babies in slings on their mothers' backs carried nothing.

Sosho raised his arms skyward, thanking the Sun God for bestowing his warmth upon them. He prayed for a bountiful summer and closed, as always, with, "We shall endure."

"We shall endure," the clan echoed.

They picked their way down the hillside path and walked across the valley to the riverbank. The roaring spring torrents sprayed the rocks they had to step on to get across.

Kono would leap from rock to rock too quickly for Malu. She took off the strap and pointed across the river. As she caught her balance on the first slippery rock, she saw Kono already sitting on the opposite bank, head cocked, as if wondering why *she* was so slow.

Under way again, the clan walked steadily—no eating, no stops. When little children became too tired to walk farther, parents carried them atop the sacks on their backs. They stopped off the trail and ran to catch up when they had to relieve themselves. Kono was pacing along so sedately, Malu decided the strap wasn't needed during the day.

Even at sunset they kept walking, and the red sky was deepening to purple before they stopped and un-strapped their burdens. Malu looked around the fast-darkening field with its huge boulders. She knew the place well, for the clan made the same stops every spring and autumn.

She helped gather brush and wood, and the fire was made. In the flickering orange light, they ate their dried food and drank from the stream that spilled among the boulders.

Though the night was chilly, the fire was not just for warmth. They needed its flames to scare off beasts that might prowl in the dark, though an animal driven by desperate hunger might attack anyway. This had happened once, when Malu was a young child.

But fears of animal attacks seemed too distant to think about. Malu was captured by the excitement of sleeping in the open, with the stars overhead and the light from the fire, surrounded by the people of her clan—and this time she'd have Kono sleeping with her, too.

Sosho called forth Gunto, for by tradition, the honor of being the firewatcher the first night went to the newest member of the hunting band. As Sosho charged him with the firewatcher's duties, to stay awake and keep the flames burning high, Gunto nodded emphatically.

"We shall endure," said Sosho.

"We shall endure," echoed the clan.

Gunto set his sacks by the fire. Malu saw him poke the fire, add wood, stand back to look at it, and sit down, moving his head constantly as if to show how alert he was. The murmur of sleepy voices fell off into silence. Kono was already asleep, her paws making tiny running steps against Malu's side. Malu watched the light of the half-round moon soften the peaks of the distant mountains to a dim edge along the dark sky.

\* \* \*

What was that! Kono growling. The strap wrenching her wrist.

Another rumbling deep growl. Malu gripped the strap with both hands.

"That wolf! Waking us up for nothing!" someone muttered.

But something was wrong. *It was dark!* No flames, no firelight!

A scream of terror. A woman's voice. "No! *No! NO!*" Scuffling noises. More screaming. Then—

*Aw-aw-awrrrrg!* The terrifying roar of a cave lion!

Hunters with spears dashed out of the circle.

Frightened voices cried out. The woman screaming and screaming. "Yubar! My baby's gone!" Dorna, Talva's mother!

Shrieking voices, jostling bodies, everyone trying to reach her. The screams became hoarse cries.

Malu choked. Not Yubar! Talva's baby brother. So little. So joyful. Just learning to talk.

"Yubar! Yubar!" Talva sobbed.

Those surrounding Dorna and Talva parted to let Sosho through with his medicine sack.

Dorna's tortured words told what had happened. So stealthily had the cave lion crept up on the sleepers that Dorna knew nothing until she felt Yubar being dragged from her arms. She struggled to hold him. The cave lion roared its fury and clawed her.

Sosho shook his head to see her arm ripped open from shoulder to elbow. She moaned over and over, "Yubar!" Talva whimpered inconsolably as Malu and Fidday tried to comfort her, Malu's tears mingling with Talva's, the memory of her own baby brother's death reawakened.

Boys had stirred the embers and set up a big blaze. There was little talk but much restless moving around. The horror of the screams and cries echoed in Malu's mind. Yubar! The first time he played with Kono on the ledge, how he had laughed when Kono licked his face.

She turned to lie on her back, staring into the night sky. The heat of anger rushed through her. Gunto—firewatcher!

As the half-moon sank into the mountains, she saw the stars grow bright, and then fade in the faint gray light before dawn.

Dim figures were straggling back. When the hunters came nearer, she saw Bromer, Talva's father, holding a bundle close to his bare chest. His deerskin shirt had become Yubar's shroud.

The hunters dug the burial hole. Malu had heard Sosho conduct the rites many times, the last being less than a year ago for her brother. Erko's coughing sickness had to run its relentless course, but Yubar's death needn't have happened. How must Talva feel!

With an angry tremor in his voice, Sosho spoke the familiar words, "How precious is the life of a chlid." This time he added, "It is a sorry time for our clan that someone's failure to keep the hunters' vows brings us here to bury this child."

The hunters began filling the burial hole to keep out animals. The *chink chink* of rock falling on rock had a dreadful finality.

This would be the end of the burial rites. But Sosho raised his hand and spoke further.

"For every broken vow there is a consequence. For Gunto, the consequence is to lose two fingers, which will mark him for life, and ever after. Bromer—your ax."

Mutilation! Malu watched as Bromer pulled the ax from his waist thong, the sharp edge glinting in the sunlight. For Gunto's fingers! What Gunto had caused was terrible, and yet she felt sorry for him.

But where *was* Gunto? She hadn't noticed his absence until now.

In silence, Sosho and the hunting band walked toward one of the boulders and disappeared behind it. Gunto must have been waiting there.

She shivered, remembering two hunters with mutilated hands. A man, now dead, had a small mutilation—one finger chopped off at the first joint. While a firewatcher, he, too, had fallen asleep and let the fire burn low, but before anything happened, he had wakened to fan the flames high.

The other was a young hunter who, while chopping a log, accidentally wounded another man. The ax blade had flown off the handle and struck the other man in the chest—a serious wound, but the man did recover. Though knowing the head of the ax was loose, the hunter had done nothing to fix it. He lost the top joints of two fingers.

Sosho and the hunters walked out from behind the boulder, their faces like stone. Gunto walked behind them. She hardly recognized his gaunt face and blankly staring eyes. His right hand held his left hand close to his chest, which rose and fell in great breaths. The left hand bulged large under wadding of dried moss bound by leather strips.

Bromer went quickly to his gear and put the ax inside his tool sack.

"It is midway to noon. Let us be on our way," said Sosho. They all shouldered their sacks and departed, Gunto alone behind the clan.

* * *

At the end of that day's march, when Zarbo was named firewatcher, Malu took Kono to him. He and Ardap sat on a rock, eating dried meat.

"Zarbo, remember last night, how Kono growled and woke us up *before* the cave lion attacked? She was warning us."

Zarbo raised his eyebrows. "Ho-la! She was—but no one understood."

"Kono could help guard us," Malu said.

"Yes." Zarbo leaned down, face to face with the wolf, and said, "Kono! Will you hear for us and smell for us? Will you warn us when danger is near?"

Kono cocked her head at him.

"That's a wolf's yes," said Zarbo, thumping Kono's chest.

Malu clasped her hands together. Kono would prove herself to the clan. She handed Kono's strap to Zarbo, and watched them walk to the fire.

Wrapped in her sleeping skin, she was happy to see her cousin and her wolf silhouetted shoulder to shoulder against the firelight. But she was lonely, too, without her wolf's furry warmth.

All was quiet that night. "She's a good watcher," Zarbo said in the morning. "Sniffing the air—sometimes she stood up and stared into the dark. She heard things I didn't hear. But there wasn't any danger to warn us about."

Malu was glad that other hunters were listening.

As they walked, with Gunto again behind the clan, the full force of how far a hunter could fall from glory suddenly struck her. The spear-throwing, the hunter's red hand, and being part of the hunting magic had

56

always glittered so bright that she'd been blind to everything else. Vows and duties—only words. Penalties—what penalties? Now, today, she saw they were grimly real.

She blew out her breath. *She* had asked Zarbo to break his vows! She shouldn't have even mentioned her taboo spear-thrower. And Ardap—he'd given her a *spear*! She slowed down to wait for Mother.

"Mother, can apprentices get mutilated like hunters?"

"No. They haven't taken hunters' vows yet. Why?"

"I just wondered."

* * *

The next days and nights passed uneventfully, and Kono sat with each firewatcher. They were coming to their last stop. It was the eighth day—a day late, because of time lost the first night. Their stomachs were grinding with hunger, for they had run out of food. Though the stony ground had given way to green plains and gentle knolls with berry bushes and fruit trees, they could not eat. The fruit was as wooden as the branches it hung from. The berries were hard green nubbins, bitter and unchewable.

Malu felt her mouth water, thinking how soft and red they'd soon be, and how the juice would tingle on her tongue as she bit into them. She could almost feel the sweet juice dribble down her chin. Soon!

She set her sleeping skin near Fidday and Talva, and they talked about living in the summer huts.

"I'm going to get so fat!" said Fidday. "I'll eat and eat. Remember the bison meat last summer?"

"I liked the ibex better," Talva said.

It was good to hear her voice. She'd hardly spoken since Yubar died. Malu reached to touch her hand.

Jubilant voices called out at the first sight of their wooded knoll, and everyone walked faster. But cheers changed to stunned cries. Running up the knoll, Malu saw a swath of destruction cut through the middle of the clearing. The huts on either side were undamaged. Those in line with Malu's hut were blown askew, and their roof hides were in shreds, but hers—it was a jumble of broken poles under a huge uprooted tree.

"We will build anew," said Father. "It will be better than before."

No, it wouldn't. She wanted her old hut, with her sleeping shelf built into a corner, and the small hole in the wall next to her head. A bush outside hid the hole so that she could look out without being seen.

In the clearing, as the clan stood around waiting for Sosho to speak, Malu heard sighs and moans. Just the way she felt—stricken.

"Some of you are old enough to remember the year fire swept through here and destroyed *all* the huts. This is not a disaster. Only one hut has to be completely rebuilt. Some huts need only a new pole or two. Roofs can be thatched. It won't take long! We shall endure!"

"We shall endure!" The echo was loud.

Sosho named the hunters who would work on the huts and those who would hunt. Women and older girls would thatch, and younger girls would watch over the little children.

Malu headed for the sandy spot where the children were already starting to play.

"Malu!" Mother called. "You're coming with us. You're old enough to learn thatching now."

Go with the women! She didn't like that! What tiresome work women did. Girls could do more exciting things. Look at Varda. Varda smiled, but where was her laugh? Did she ever say, like last spring, "Let's be the first ones to go in the river?" And would she ever whisper, "Let's try again to find the Magic Chamber"? No! She was only pretending to like being a woman.

As Malu followed the women, she saw Varda far ahead, and began wondering when Varda's marriage would be arranged, and if her husband would be someone outside the clan. She hoped not.

Marriage was the worst part of being a woman. Soon Varda would meet her *husband*. She'd have to go and live with him in *his* clan. Leave all her friends. Maybe never see her mother and father again.

Mother's birth clan was the Tall Trees. She'd told

Malu about saying good-bye to her parents and her clan. A few years later, a seashell trader had stopped at the Tall Trees clan on his way to the Cliff clan. As he displayed his beautiful shells here, he brought word of clans where he'd been trading. Malu remembered how Mother had cried when he told her that *her* mother was dead, and her father had married Mother's aunt.

Malu drew in her breath. What if this happened to *her*? Leave Mother and Father, Zarbo and Ardap, Sosho? Leave Fidday and Talva? Varda would already be gone. Never see the Clan of the Cliff again, and the mountains and woods and valley and river—and the summer huts? No. She wanted everything just the way it was *now*!

Mother turned to look back at her, and smiled. Suddenly she saw Mother as she'd never seen her before. Her smile—her face, rosy and moist with the heat, the way she pushed a loose strand of hair off her face—not just Mother—a girl like herself. She felt something burst inside her.

Catching up, she held Mother's hand, and walking between her and Kono, Malu felt better. If only it could always stay this way.

At the plain, Malu knelt in the stiff, tawny grass, watching the women cut it. They pulled a handful of grass tight from the ground with one hand, and with a quick slash of the knife cut through it. That looked easy enough.

Malu tried to copy the women exactly, but her knife

didn't slash through it. She hacked at it four more times to free it. She shook her hand. The sharp edges of the grass blades cut into her fingers. Gritting her teeth, she kept at it. After cutting grass all morning, she was working faster. When the women said they had enough, she pressed her sore fingers together, whispering, "At last!"

"We'll bundle the grass in the clearing," said Fidday's mother. As they started dragging their sacks of grass up the knoll, Malu heard excited voices call out from those ahead. "Look at the huts!"

Almost running with her sack, Malu saw freshly cut poles standing erect near the fallen tree—the skeleton of her new hut! And the other huts were standing straight now with their poles. The day was not so bad after all. She closed her eyes thankfully.

As the girls watched the women start bundling the cut grass, they complained about their cut fingers.

"Come, come! You have soft baby hands," said Fidday's mother, holding a hand palm up. "After you've worked more, you'll have nice hard hands like mine."

Malu nodded. Mother's hands were like that—so leathery even sharp thorns didn't hurt. She hoped it wouldn't take much longer to get tough hands.

Copying the women, Malu lined up a bunch of grass to lie all in one direction, and twisted a few grass blades into a strand for tying them. These bundles would be fastened, overlapping, to the roof poles. Making bundles looked easy—but so had the cutting.

She wasn't surprised when the grass blades kept sticking to her sweaty hands. And when the knot wouldn't stay tied. Hissing out her breath, she tied one good bundle at last. The next one went faster, and soon she began feeling a rhythm in her motions. Compared to the cutting, this was almost fun.

That night, Malu and her parents laid their sleeping skins within the framework of their new hut. Rubbing her sore fingers, she looked up through the roof poles at the stars. Tomorrow night, with the thatching in place, the blood of her fingers would be part of the roof.

Boar meat is the best meat of all," said Malu. With the fat running down her chin, she gnawed on her second great chunk. Father and Mother nodded and licked their fingers.

The clan was feasting after the day's hunt. All afternoon the girls had been at the big hearth in the clearing, turning the green-wood spits that held the big haunches of boar.

Malu chewed her last bite and patted her full belly. It was wonderful to eat until you could eat no more! When was their last feast? Too long ago to remember.

She looked over the scraps of meat and bones and gathered the best ones for Kono. She ran to the tree where she'd tied up her wolf.

"Here's *your* feast!" Kono was already standing up, nose sniffing, eyes shining. She gulped down the first piece before it touched the ground. Malu laughed. She loved watching Kono eat.

After the sun set, she went to the new hut. Father and the other men had rebuilt almost all of the damaged huts, and even Malu's hut was finished except for the sleeping shelves.

She stretched out on the ground with Kono. Tonight, instead of stars overhead, thatching covered the roof—*her* thatching. During the night she awoke to the drip-drip of rain falling off the thatch outside. Her thatch was good. She felt snug and proud.

When the boar meat was nearly gone, the hunters set out, and brought back two red deer. They ate well, but Father said red deer were hard to find this summer. Ibex, though, looked promising. Several times they had been spotted in the distance.

During the next moon, many plants came into ripeness. And so it was that each morning, while the hunters went seeking big game, Malu and the other girls went to the big storage hut, where the women told them what to pick.

"Out there near the berries, the pods are ripe now," said Mother. Malu, Talva, and Fidday each took a sack and found the pod vines.

Kono lay down nearby as Malu knelt by the plants, quickly pulling off the full green pods and dropping them in the sack. When she'd picked all the pods she could reach, she moved farther along on her knees. Only a moon ago, picking pods would have hurt her hands, but now they were almost as hard as Mother's. But her knees ached. Maybe she needed hard knees, too. She sat back on her heels to rest.

She made a face. She knew plant food was important for the clan. But hunting was *exciting*—the chase, and wondering what was going to happen! Here, with the plants, it was just pick, pick, pick, and cut, cut, cut.

She could just see herself out there, *really* hunting with a spear—not shooting stones with a slingshot, like babies. Scanning the distance, tracking and stalking with Kono at her side. Then *seeing* an actual ibex or bison, circling around it downwind, and getting close enough to aim, lunge, and *whoosh!*—her spear soaring straight to the heart. A kill! *Ho-la!*

She looked at the pod in her hand. Pod picking! *Hoo!* She wanted to smash it. Kono sat up and cocked her head.

"You know how it is, don't you, Kono. We should both be hunting!"

Kono whined. She knew.

Malu dropped the pod into her sack and went on picking.

*   *   *

"I don't see why we have to keep on and on with this." Talva wiped her hand across her sweaty brow. "Aren't the women ever going to say, 'That's enough'?"

"I wonder," Malu said. "I think we already have more dried food than we got all last summer."

"They'll never say 'Enough,'" said Fidday, rolling her eyes. She opened a pod. "These beans don't taste bad."

"But look at the berries over there. Let's eat *them*." Talva dropped her sack, and Malu and Fidday followed her. The dimpled red berries were a little tart, but so good!

Kono looked as if she were waiting for a taste. "Here! See how you like it," Malu said, tossing a berry at her. When Kono sniffed it in midair and let it fall, they laughed.

From here Malu could see the women on the sunny side of the big storage hut. They never seemed to laugh or stop to rest or eat bits of the food. As some washed and sliced the food gathered yesterday, others set it out to dry in the sun. In the afternoon, before dew moistened the dried food, everyone, girls and women, hastened to carry it into the storage hut.

After filling her sack with pods, Malu dragged it to the drying field. Two women on hands and knees were turning over half-dried slices of fruit.

"The gods have granted us many sunny days," said one of the women. "We'll have more dried food than last winter."

The other nodded. "A good thing, too. If only this winter the mammoths would come back! If they don't— Oh, Malu, what a fine sack of pods. Next you can start digging the roots over there beyond the berries."

Malu nodded and picked up a sack. She felt numb. She'd never thought there'd be another winter without mammoths! Until last winter, the mammoths had always come.

In the cold clutch of winter, mammoth was the clan's one reliable big game. Without mammoth, they had some goats and boars, but mostly small game, such as Malu had hunted with slingshot and stones. Last winter it was the dried plant food from summer's bounty that made up the difference and let the clan endure.

In autumn the hoofed animals, like deer, would flee to faraway lands, where—she had heard—the earth was barren in summer, but lush in winter when the rains came.

A land that was warm in winter? She hadn't believed it until Sosho himself told her.

"Why don't *we* go there?" she'd asked.

"It's too far away, Malu," he said, laughing. "Did you ever try to run with a deer?"

"I wouldn't even try—they're so fast," she had answered. Sosho often asked questions that at first seemed silly, but they never were.

"Of course. Deer and the other herd animals can run fast enough to flee south from winter's cold, and then flee north from the barren summer. How far do you think *we* could travel? Half a year to get there, and the other half to get back? We'd have to travel all the time—we couldn't have a home."

Not have a home! Then they wouldn't even *be* the Clan of the Cliff.

She remembered this, walking toward the root plants. The women's talk of mammoths—they were probably right. Another winter of hunger. But with enough plant food, not starvation.

She struck her digging flint into the ground, pulling out fat yellow roots one after another, not stopping to look up or talk.

\* \* \*

The hunters were ready to go at dawn one morning, heading west, where they'd spotted ibex in the distance the day before. With others standing at the top of the knoll, Malu and Kono were watching them leave. Zarbo stopped when he saw Malu, and Kono leaped at him, setting her paws on his shoulders.

He thumped her deep chest like a drum. "This wolf wants to hunt!"

"She'll track those ibex," said Malu. "Take her along!"

"I will—someday." Laughing, he ran on.

Gunto rushed along among the others, taking great long strides, his eyes fixed straight ahead. His spear-thrower and the shaft of his spear gleamed from being rubbed with bear fat. He was forever honing and polishing his gear, when he wasn't practicing with his spear-thrower.

"Look at him, all shining bright," said Fidday.

"I guess now he's trying to do everything right," said Malu. She wasn't used to him this way. She almost missed his loud bragging and boasting.

Going on to the storage hut, the girls took empty sacks and spent another day gathering plant food.

After the dried food was put in the storage hut and the sun dropped low in the west, the hunters had not returned. One by one, the girls went to the crest of the knoll to watch for them. Voices fell silent as all who sat in the clearing listened for the hoped-for cry that the hunters were coming.

Women started walking to the crest. Kono stood up, looking intently at the watchers. Soon everyone stood there.

Something must have happened. Everyone knew it. But to avoid tempting fate, no one spoke of fear.

"I think I see them!" a girl called out.

From behind a slope of the plain, runners were coming.

A woman, shading her eyes against the sun, shrilled, "I see three hunters running ahead. Carrying someone! Someone's wounded!"

Staring into the setting sun, Malu couldn't quite make out the figures. *Don't let it be Father!*

The runners came steadily closer. Of the small advance group, she saw Ardap, ahead. Behind him, the two carrying someone. Father—safe! The other, Olik, Zarbo's father.

*Zarbo!* A tremor went through her. Zarbo, wounded!

Soon Ardap stumbled up the knoll, carrying the gear of the others, and fell to the ground. "Zarbo—hurt bad—kicked by an elk!"

As Father and Olik rushed by, Malu glimpsed Zarbo's closed eyes and ashen face. She, Mother, and Laris—Zarbo's mother—followed them into Sosho's hut. They gently laid Zarbo on Sosho's sleeping shelf.

Sosho held up Zarbo's head to help him drink a sleeping potion. Zarbo's eyes closed when Sosho unwrapped bloody moss from the wound, just below the knee. As he cleaned the wound, Malu saw a deep gash and the jagged edge of a broken bone. She held back a sob and turned away. Mother, who was learning to become a healer, did Sosho's bidding as he prepared to fit the two ends of bone together. He asked the others to leave, for Zarbo would not waken until morning.

They joined the rest of the clan in the clearing, where the hunters were halfheartedly skinning and butchering the ibexes, and cutting slices for quick cooking over the fire. No one made a move to roast them. Ardap sat leaning against a rock nearby, looking pale and weary.

Sosho came out. "Eat! It's your duty to keep strong!"

As they started roasting the meat, Ardap haltingly

told how he and Zarbo had gone off together on their own. They had each got an ibex, and were in a hollow, starting to skin them. Suddenly Zarbo leaped to his feet.

"An elk!" he had cried out, grabbing a spear and dashing over the rise.

"Come back! We already have too much to carry!" Ardap had shouted, but Zarbo paid no heed.

Standing up, Ardap had glimpsed Zarbo stalking a browsing elk, circling it, and disappearing behind a rolling slope. Loath to leave the ibexes to scavengers, Ardap waited for Zarbo to come back, sure that he'd quickly regain his sense.

He'd kept waiting. Finally he went searching. There was nothing to see but vultures flying toward a spot in the distance. With a feeling of dread, he ran toward it. Zarbo was lying on the ground, encircled by vultures that were jostling for position, watching for the moment of death. Zarbo was weakly waving his hand to ward them off.

Ardap had dashed at them, swinging his spear. They backed up into a wider circle. He took care of Zarbo as well as he could, hoping the hunters would soon find them. When they did, Father and Olik hastily made a litter of skins and carried Zarbo off.

"What about the elk?" asked a boy.

It had disappeared before Ardap arrived. As for the ibexes, when Ardap and the others passed them, vultures were already devouring them.

*  *  *

Malu, entering Sosho's hut the next morning, found Olik kneeling by the sleeping shelf. Laris, wiping her eyes, drew Malu aside.

"Sosho joined his broken bone. The leg will heal, but he can't even wiggle his toes. My son! He's going to be lame!" she whispered. "He has the death wish, and nothing we say will stop him from dying. You try, Malu."

What could she say? Malu stretched her lips into a smile. "Zarbo, I—I— Heal fast, Zarbo. You *will* get well."

"No. Can't hunt, leaning on a stick. I will die." He turned his face to the wall.

Laris and Olik talked to Zarbo. Malu's parents talked to him. Malu talked to him again, and so did Ardap and Sosho. To all he said he would die. Finally he kept his face turned away and would not answer.

Sosho sighed and said softly, "Zarbo, what you told me about chasing the elk—do you want to tell them? Or should I?"

"I will." He looked at them. "Then maybe you'll understand and let me die in peace."

He seemed to be looking into himself, describing his vision. "Biggest elk I ever saw. Got my spear, chased him. Threw it—pierced his haunch and hung there. He staggered on. I caught up. Didn't have my other spear to finish him off. I yanked to pull out the spear. He kicked me."

A great weariness seemed to come over him. "Animal Master was generous—already had more meat than we needed. But when I saw the elk"—he closed his eyes—"bloodlust made me do it. Animal Master punished me. Can never hunt again."

This was terrible! The death wish! Malu knew Zarbo. If he decided to die, he would die.

Ardap leaned forward. "Live for us, Zarbo."

"Can't hunt. Can't live like a woman."

Clustered around the sleeping shelf, they all begged and wheedled, groping for words—any words to change his mind!

"Leave me alone!" he muttered.

Couldn't anyone make him want to live? She looked to Sosho, her only hope. Tears in *his* eyes!

Zarbo stirred and looked at them. "What happened to my spear-thrower?"

She felt a lift of hope. If he was interested in that—!

"I brought it back home for you. I'll get it." Ardap ran out and quickly reappeared.

Zarbo held the spear-thrower, tracing the shape of the horse with his finger, touching the lines he'd incised for its nostrils, eyes, and mane. Malu remembered watching him make it, the pains he took, carving and polishing, and cutting the lines of the mane just so.

"I bequeath my spear-thrower to Malu." His voice was firm.

Malu felt shivery hot.

"Hunters pass on their spear-throwers to another hunter, Grandson," Sosho said gently.

"Malu throws spear. She hunts."

Sosho looked at her. She bowed her head.

"So be it. Take it, Malu."

She slowly put out her hand. But to take it was like agreeing to his death. She mustn't!

"Look at this, Zarbo!" she said. "See the mane blowing in the wind—the flaring nostrils—how hard it's been running! You gave this horse life. If you die, it will be just a piece of bone."

"It will live when you hunt with it."

"Zarbo," said Sosho, "I must see this!" He took it from Zarbo and turned it over, looking closely at the horse. He looked up, his eyes gleaming. "Ardap, go to Ullas! Tell him our search is over!"

Ardap ran out again, looking as puzzled as Malu felt.

Sosho tapped his finger on the spear-thrower. "You, Zarbo! You'll learn Ullas's magic and become the next image-maker!"

"What do you mean?" Anger tinged Zarbo's voice.

"No one has been told yet. Listen, my grandson." Sosho talked fast. "Ullas's eyes are fast clouding over. His image-making days are few. We knew we must find an apprentice for him before it is too late. We've seen no one else in the clan who has the eye and the hand of an image-maker. Until today. The one who made this horse—you, Zarbo—you!"

"No!"

"You will work with Ullas and learn his image-making magic."

"No."

"A clan without an image-maker is a hungry clan. We need you."

"Leave me alone!"

As Ullas rushed in, Sosho handed him the spear-thrower. "Behold Zarbo's skill!"

A wide smile lit Ullas's face. "Zarbo—my apprentice! What a blessing!"

"No, no," Zarbo whispered.

Ullas turned questioning eyes toward Sosho.

"Ullas and I will talk alone with Zarbo," said Sosho. "I must ask the rest of you to leave now."

Exchanging hopeful glances, they left.

Feeling anxious, Malu took Kono for a walk. Zarbo was so unpredictable. On her return, she saw the joy in everyone's face. She went to her sleeping shelf and cried. He would live!

Later, Sosho gave Malu the spear-thrower. "This is yours now. Another time we will talk about your hunting."

* * *

When the healing was complete, Zarbo would not leave the sleeping shelf. One day Malu went to Sosho's door and heard Sosho's voice.

"It is time, Zarbo, for you to start using your leg."

When Zarbo answered in an angry mutter, she went away.

She was sitting with Zarbo the next day as Ardap entered and without a word gave him a forked stick he'd made from a sturdy tree limb. She feared Zarbo would fly into a rage, but he grimly set it against the wall within reach.

To her surprise, a few days later he was leaning on the stick, walking around the clearing, cursing himself when his limp foot dragged on the ground. He was so intense, no one dared speak to him.

Never referring to his injury, Zarbo soon swung along with his stick as if it had always been a part of him. She admired his spirit. But to see her cousin like this—who'd been the clan's best hunter and thrown the farthest, truest spear—pained her mightily. She wondered if she'd ever hear his laugh ring out again.

\* \* \*

Sosho soon had his talk with Malu. "I understand you made yourself a spear-thrower. How did that come about?"

She told him about finding the antler and seeing the wolf image in it. "I was going to make it just the

76

image of a wolf, but it was the perfect shape for a spear-thrower, and I—just finished it."

"I'd like to see it."

He held it up and looked at it. "A fine spear-thrower. And you've used it?"

She told him everything. How she had spied on the boys in the practice field to learn throwing spear. How Ardap had helped her, not Zarbo. Why hunting with sling and stones was no longer a challenge. How she'd always longed to take the next step—throwing spear.

Sosho nodded, but looked puzzled. "Malu, I worry about you. Does a boy's spirit live in your girl's body? Do you forget your destiny—to become a woman, not a hunter?"

"No, I don't forget it." She spoke fast. "Someday—someday I must marry and have babies. I can't be a boy or go on the Hunt of Passage or be initiated or have the red hand."

"Then what is it you want, Granddaughter?"

She took a deep breath. "I want to be a girl with a spear-thrower—a girl who hunts."

Sosho raised her chin with his fingertips and looked at her. Then he looked into the distance. He was having a vision. She sat stiffly upright, until, blinking fast, he looked at her again.

"*Be* a girl who hunts, Malu. In due time the clan will be told. Ardap, Zarbo, and I—does anyone else know of this?"

"Only Mother and Father, and Laris and Olik,

because they were there when Zarbo gave me the spear-thrower."

"Oh, yes." Sosho stood up.

"Sosho . . . Grandfather . . ." Words wouldn't come. She reached for his hand and pressed it to her cheek.

"Off with you now—Girl Who Hunts!"

# CHAPTER SIX

Malu stirred in and out of a dream. She was at the winter caves, running barefoot in the snow, and shivering in her sleeveless summer tunic. She blinked awake. The shivering felt so real! It *was* real, and a cold wind was blowing through the hut. She saw Mother wearing a long shirt over her tunic.

"How could it be so cold, Mother?"

"It looks like an early winter, and we may have to go back to the caves. Sosho is talking to the hunters."

Wrapping her sleeping skin about her, Malu ran across the cold dirt floor to the doorway and saw dark clouds swirling across the sky. The hunters were leaving Sosho's hut, and Father walked briskly toward her.

"We go tomorrow," he said. "If it snows while we're here, we might never get out."

"We'd freeze!" Mother put her hand to the wall palings, spaced to let summer breezes cool the hut.

To keep warm, Malu put on all her summer clothing, layer on layer. They spent the day getting ready. Malu went to the storage hut, where each person was taking a sack of the dried food to carry back to the caves.

Malu strapped on her sacks the next morning, laughing to see Kono already at the doorway, panting eagerly.

Walking down the knoll, Malu looked back at the hut. It was a good hut, as good as the old one, after all. She hoped it would still be there next spring.

The morning sun warmed her. But as the day ended, she shivered, even bundled up as she was. She needed the wolf's furry warmth next to her. She didn't want Kono to sit with the firewatcher. After all, her growls would rouse the clan just as well if she slept by Malu. Everyone agreed, and Malu was warm on even the coldest night.

During the third night, Kono's growls sent the hunters leaping to circle around the clan with their spears. After a cautious wait, the hunters returned to their sleeping skins.

As they began walking in the morning, Zarbo called out, "Cave lion!" and pointed to scat with dirt scuffed over it.

"Maybe the fire kept the lion away," said Bromer, "and maybe not. But Kono guards us well. She gives us time we might need to defend ourselves." His words carried weight, for no one could forget Yubar's fate.

\* \* \*

Everyone walking near Malu stopped to praise and pet Kono. Kono began leaping exuberantly, and Malu stepped off the trail to put the strap on her. The heavy sack of food on Malu's back had shifted, so, letting the others walk ahead, she took time to balance her load better.

Suddenly Kono yelped and almost tore the strap off Malu's wrist. Whirling around, Malu saw Gunto switching his spear to his left hand.

"What's bothering that wolf?" he said, swerving wide as he strode by.

"You leave her alone!" Malu said. He laughed and walked faster.

Furiously, she ran her fingers through Kono's coat, feeling for a wound. No wound, but the jab of a spear could bruise without piercing the wolf's skin.

Malu gritted her teeth, remembering the night of Gunto's initiation, how he had spat at her—and Zarbo's warning. Now Gunto was getting at her through her wolf.

\* \* \*

After crossing the river on the seventh day, tired from walking and trying to keep warm, Malu saw the cliff of their caves looming ahead. Home! Though her spirit was racing up there to touch the rocky ledge, she couldn't make her body run.

On the Great Ledge the hunters made a fire to light torches, and searched the caves. Malu was thankful they found no animals. After a hasty meal of dried food and water in the Clan Hall, they walked along the ledge toward their own caves.

Kono's claws clicked on the rocky surface as she sniffed her way along, leading Malu and her parents. The wolf stopped at their cave and looked up at her.

"You remember everything, don't you!" Malu patted Kono's head as they went inside. Letting their sacks fall to the floor, they pulled out their warm bear skins and climbed onto their sleeping shelves. Malu flung her arm over Kono and closed her eyes, feeling warm and snug for the first time since summer's sudden end.

She hurried to the lookout in the morning to see the wolves, fearing that Old Wolf might have died during the summer.

But there she was, alone. At Malu's footsteps, Old Wolf turned her head upward, and Malu saw that her eyes were now milky white.

"Poor Old Wolf," she murmured, "you can't even see now."

Old Wolf suddenly pointed her nose toward the river, and Malu shifted her gaze. Though blind, Old

Wolf had sensed the pack was coming. They were as Malu always pictured them in her mind, strung out in a line, heavy bodies slung on long, lean legs, trotting at a smooth, easy pace.

Black Chief, barely glancing at Malu, sniffed a circle around his favorite hollow and lay down. The others found their special spots and groaned great yawns as they settled down. Last came Gray Wolf, a chunk of meat swinging from her jaws.

Strange! Gray Wolf had no young ones to feed. Curious, Malu watched Gray Wolf trot over to Old Wolf and drop the meat at her muzzle. Old Wolf licked it and raised her head toward Gray Wolf, their eyes fixed on each other as if both could see. Then Gray Wolf lay down near Black Chief, head between her paws.

"Gray Wolf feeding Old Wolf!" Malu whispered to herself.

Wolves! The more she knew of them, the more they surprised her. She ran home, eager to tell someone about Gray Wolf, someone who cared about wolves.

Fidday and Talva were not in sight. Ardap was off with the hunters. In the Clan Hall, Zarbo was peering at some seeds in his hand as Ullas talked about paint colors. Then Varda walked in, and Malu told her.

Varda clasped her hands. "A wolf doing that!"

"Varda, I wonder if Old Wolf is—"

"If Old Wolf is Gray Wolf's mother!" They looked at each other, wide-eyed. Then one of the women called to Varda, and she crossed the Clan Hall to the women's benches. Though Varda sat there as a woman among women, she was still Varda.

* * *

Tiny snowflakes whirled about like icy petals in the wind, and the sun was only a pale glow behind thick gray clouds. Snow already? It wasn't even close to the turn of the year.

Malu watched the hunters set out. Bundled in their fur clothes, bristling with spears and axes and knives, they looked like strange hulking beasts. Since they'd be up in the mountains hunting for goats, she was free to throw spear today. How she longed to see her spear go flying!

But first she had to carry the trash down to the lookout. The pack was gone again. She scanned the grounds for Old Wolf. It was hard to spot her sometimes, her tan coat a close match to autumn's faded grass. Then a splash of red, like fresh-spilt blood, caught her eye.

It *was* blood. Oozing from Old Wolf's belly. Old Wolf lay there, a lump of pale fur.

She ran down into the hollow. Who had killed Old Wolf? She wiped her eyes to see better. Five separate puncture wounds. No mauling by claws or fangs, these. No slashing to open up the flesh. *Spear wounds!*

A hunter had stabbed Old Wolf. Malu was rigid

with outrage. Who had done this? Someone who had always spoken ill of wolves. Who poked his spear at her strong wolf only when Kono was held by a strap. Who found a sick, old, blind wolf that he *could* spear to death.

"You big, brave hunter!" she shouted. But there was no one to hear. She drew deep breaths until she could stop shaking.

Footprints! She looked, but the hard ground and flying flakes of snow revealed nothing. Poor Old Wolf. Though she wouldn't have lived much longer, she had been cared for. This was the wrong way for Old Wolf to die.

She must tell Sosho! She ran up the path. He wasn't in the Clan Hall, but Zarbo was.

"Gunto killed Old Wolf!" she said. "I want to tell Sosho!"

Zarbo listened as she told him what she'd seen. "I know how you feel. I don't like it, either. But Sosho can't do anything about it."

"Even though Gunto killed a helpless animal for no reason?"

"We think we know that," Zarbo said. "You can tell Sosho, but he'll ask how you can prove it."

"I'm going to tell him anyway," said Malu.

She found Sosho at midday, and it was as Zarbo had predicted. Except that Sosho frowned and said, "I respect your opinion, Malu."

She'd done all she could for Old Wolf. She went

to the practice field with Kono, but the spear did not fly well today. Old Wolf was too heavy on her mind. She took a walk with Kono, almost to the river, giving her a chance to romp and run. Kono's antics kept her from hugging her sadness to herself.

"Ho-la! Ho-la!" The hunters' shouts echoed down the mountain. By the time Malu reached the Clan Hall, the younger hunters were already skinning the goat carcasses, butchering the flesh, scraping hides clean, chiseling off the curved horns. They set aside the unbroken ones, to be made into vials for Sosho's potions, or fashioned for blowing music.

Children screeched and raced around. Some played with a carcass, shaking the horns, tugging at the shaggy hair, screaming and giggling. A little boy bumped into Malu, and she held his arm to keep him from falling. He looked up at her, laughing, and ran off. She watched him. She used to be like him, thinking of nothing more than play.

After the goat feast, she spotted Ardap sitting alone, turning a goat horn over and over in his hands, looking at it from all sides, for he was a blower of music. Why, he and she were alike. She had looked at the antler and seen the wolf image inside, and shaped it so the wolf could emerge. Now he was listening to the tones within the horn, and would shape it to let the music blow out.

\*    \*    \*

The snows came, but lightly. Malu practiced throwing spear whenever the hunters were away, and she was doing well now. When the spear soared straight to the farthest log and bit into it with a solid *thunk*, instead of bouncing off, she danced on her toes. Her throwing arm had become much stronger. She flexed her muscles. How big and hard they were now! The work of last summer must have done this for her. Maybe her spear could pierce the hide of a bison or bear. She must strike those logs again and again!

As real winter blustered in, the bountiful hunts that had given the clan deer feasts, and ibex and goat feasts, were no more. The mountain goats hadn't disappeared, but they easily bounded away on snow-covered rocks where hunters stumbled and fell.

Though Malu liked the meat of birds and small game, many in the clan said they never had full bellies, and ate that much more of the dried food. The women talked of their worry that without big game, the dried food would not last the winter.

The turning point of the year, the shortest day, was gloomier than usual. From darkness at morning until afternoon dusk the clan fasted and prayed, for without their prayers, the gods might forget to let the sun shine longer each day, so that spring could come and new life start.

With dusk came the solstice feast. Malu bit off big chunks of goose. She chewed the rich, fatty meat, swirling her tongue around her lips to catch the juice dripping down her chin. She laughed to see Kono doing the same, except that the wolf's big tongue did it better. After eating her fill, Malu licked the tasty grease off her fingers to savor the very last bit. In spite of everything, it was a great solstice feast.

As they sat around afterward, Malu heard hunters praising Zarbo for the picture of a mammoth he was painting on the wall of the Magic Chamber. He said little, but his eyes glinted, and she realized his strained look had eased into the zestful face she used to see. How wise Sosho had been: He who had carved the horse spear-thrower had become enthralled with image-making.

She longed to see the painting. A futile wish for a girl, she knew. The Magic Chamber—taboo. But the anger didn't rise in her chest as before, for Sosho had called her Girl Who Hunts.

\* \* \*

The hunters sat around the hearth to plan another search for mammoths. As they honed a spear-thrower or chipped a fine edge on spearpoint or ax, they spun tales of past hunts. Malu and the others sat with them, listening.

"What do you do on a mammoth hunt?" a young apprentice asked. Malu looked into the wisps of smoke drifting up to the high vaulted ceiling, trying to imagine what a whole, living mammoth was like.

She knew mammoths by their parts. She had eaten mammoth meat. She had heard the deep booming of a drum made from a mammoth's pelvic bone. She had run her hand over a mammoth's huge curved tusk, and the smooth, warm beads of Mother's ivory necklace. She had felt the coarse hair of a mammoth pelt, and her fingers had pinched the mammoth's thick, tough hide.

". . . Tusker," said Sosho. That was the word she was listening for. She leaned closer, eager to hear more about the matriarch who led the herd, a wise and ancient mammoth.

"On my first mammoth hunt, when I was younger than Ardap," said Sosho, "Tusker still had two good tusks. The next winter she had the half-tusk and the ripped ear. We used to wonder what happened to her." He paused reflectively.

"I remember that hunt," said Ullas. "The young mammoths running around on the plain, near the gorge, and the mothers trying to quiet them, so they could go down the steep path to the river. Tusker always led the way down, to keep them from going too fast."

Sosho leaned forward, talking fast, his eyes gleaming, and in the flickering firelight, Malu glimpsed the young hunter he had been then. "This time, our hunting band circled around the back of the herd without being noticed. Then we made great noise, shouting and whooping and banging our spears and drum, and scared the young ones into running away from us, and toward the gorge.

"Then old Tusker saw what we were up to. She ran around bellowing and swinging her trunk at them, trying to lead them *away* from the gorge. But the herd was in a panic, the ones behind pushing the ones ahead. I think it was ten mammoths that fell over the edge and died."

Malu tried to picture the huge hairy beasts tumbling down into the gorge. What a sight it must have been!

"It was the easiest hunt I can remember, and not one of us got wounded." Ullas patted his belly. "And that one hunt gave us meat for the whole winter. We took home what we could carry, and the rest froze so hard, the vultures could only peck chips off it. When we needed more meat, we just went back and hacked off more."

The hunters fell silent, gazing into the flames. They, like her, must be seeing mammoths and wishing they'd be as lucky as the young Sosho and Ullas. Kono snuffled in her sleep and laid her head in Malu's lap.

To Malu's surprise, Zarbo spoke. Since he was no longer a hunter, he usually said little. "I've been trying to think what we—you, I mean—could do. Something we never did before."

"Zarbo's right—it's got to be something different."

Gunto snorted his explosive laugh. "What could that be? We've already searched in all directions!"

"But only as far as we could go and get back in two or three days," said Bromer. "Let's try a *long* search! Take more food—walk two days, search two days— and two days to come home."

"We can do that!"

"Let's do it!"

"But there's no meat here now for the women and children," a hunter said.

Several women spoke at once, and others nodded. "We still have bones for broth. . . ." "And our plant food. . . ." "We can hunt with our slingshots. . . ."

"I don't like leaving the caves unprotected all that time," said an older hunter. "Remember the cave lion we found prowling on the ledge? It takes spears to kill a beast like that. Maybe one of us should stay here."

"But we need *all* the hunters and apprentices," said Bromer. "You don't often find mammoths at the edge of a gorge. They're likely to be on the open plain."

"Bromer's right," said Sosho. "The most dangerous animals to hunt are mammoths out in the open. I've seen many good hunters trampled to death."

As they paused, Zarbo again broke his silence. "You can all go. Malu throws spear. And she'll have Kono to sniff out any animals that might be lurking about."

There was a strange silence, as if suddenly everyone in the Clan Hall had stopped breathing.

"You must be jesting, Zarbo!" said a hunter.

"We would have seen her throwing spear," another added.

Malu felt a wild pulsing inside. All those eyes glinting at her in the firelight! She looked up at the ceiling, wishing she could melt into the smoke and vanish.

"What Zarbo says is true," said Sosho. "He bequeathed his spear-thrower to Malu. Any hunter departing from the hunting band, for whatever reason, can make such a gift."

"But he gave it to a *girl*!" Gunto snarled.

"Why did you, Zarbo?" The man's voice was harsh.

Zarbo spoke calmly. "Because she has the heart of a hunter."

Again—silence. Malu sat up straight. She laid her hand on Kono's ruff, feeling her powerful neck. Whatever the hunters were going to say, she was proud of Zarbo's words and Sosho's trust. And of Kono, her strong friend.

"Can't have girls in our hunting band!" said a hunter. Heads nodded, and voices murmured agreement.

"Those who want to hunt with spear and spear-thrower can do so," said Sosho, "but they won't be in the hunting band."

"Well," said Bromer gruffly, "I didn't like the idea much at first, but having more hunters isn't bad, is it? Maybe have their own hunting band?"

Gunto snorted again, but said nothing.

Malu heard further mutterings, but she'd expected

worse. No matter what happened now, she didn't have to hide things anymore. She felt free.

Already the hunters' voices were rising excitedly again, planning their long search. They would leave at dawn.

* * *

As Malu drank her bone broth, Father pushed through the door flap with another load of firewood. "I must go to the Clan Hall now. We're leaving soon."

Malu rarely missed prayers for the safe return of departing hunters. Didn't it make sense, that the prayers of many people would win favor with the gods, more than the prayers of just a few? Today of all days she must be there.

After "We shall endure," she and Kono ran down to a boulder at the end of the ledge, standing at the far side, where she could see but not be seen by the hunters as they turned down the hillside path. They were already streaming by, and there was Father, running fast, his gear strapped on his back, his eyes steady on the valley below. After he disappeared around the bend, she remained watching, to see him again as the hunters reappeared below in the valley. What a long six days it would be—the waiting and not knowing.

There were voices coming from the ledge, angry voices, coming closer.

"I couldn't help it!" Gunto shouted.

Closer still. Sosho's was the other voice.

"You *can* help it. The others wake up when they should. We'll take this up when you come back."

Heavy feet pounding closer. Gunto coming. Mustn't let him see her.

Pulling Kono's strap tight, she pressed against the boulder. He was running by, back straps flapping loose, arms reaching behind, struggling with his jumble of hunting gear. His face red, eyes flashing with anger.

He hadn't seen her. Then Kono growled.

He gripped his spear and jerked to a stop. "Oh, it's Malu! Going to save the whole clan with her little spear!"

She glared at him, vowing not to answer.

He sneered. "A girl *trying* to be a hunter!"

Malu felt fire inside. "At least *I* know when not to *sleep!*"

He flung himself down the path, shouting, "You'll be sorry, Malu!"

# CHAPTER SEVEN

Entering the cave, Malu dragged her feet. When she saw Sosho there, talking with Mother, she felt shaky inside.

Mother looked up. "Why, Malu, where have you been since the hunters left?"

"On the path, watching them leave. Then Gunto came along, and he saw me." She looked at Sosho. His sharp glance made her falter. "He—he said some bad things to me, and I answered him back."

"How did this come about?" asked Sosho.

She sat on the floor with Kono. "I was behind the boulder. I wanted to watch Father till he ran out of sight. Then I heard Gunto shouting, and what you said to him. I didn't want Gunto to see me, but when he went by, Kono growled at him."

She'd have to tell them everything. . . .

When she'd finished, Sosho's eyes were the icy blue

that struck fear into her. "Gunto was very foolish. But you were foolish, too, Malu."

"I know." She bowed her head.

Sosho said nothing more to her, but, turning to Mother, talked awhile about healing powders, and left. Malu felt uneasy. She had disappointed Sosho. And Gunto—he was so hot-tempered. If only she had stuck to what she'd intended—say nothing!

* * *

Five more days until the hunters would come back from their long search. Would Father or Ardap or Olik be wounded? Would the hunters find the mammoths? People talked little about their worries, but Malu saw pinched faces and frowns, and tempers grew short.

Malu was restless, walking about in the snow with Kono, and later, taking what little refuse there was down to the lookout. The wolves weren't there. She couldn't talk to Zarbo, for he was in the Magic Chamber—as usual, when she wanted to see him. She didn't see Sosho, either—but she wasn't sure she wanted to. Nothing was as she wanted it to be.

The one certain thing in her life was Kono. Kono never said "shouldn't." She never questioned why Malu did what she did, or said what she said. To Kono, everything Malu did was right.

While picking her way along the snowy ledge with Kono, she saw Fidday.

"I've been looking for you, Malu!" Fidday lowered her voice. "Could you show me how to throw spear?"

Malu nodded. "Yes! Let's start right now while there's no one around—up in the practice field."

Malu showed Fidday how to hold and balance the spear and thrower in her right hand. Malu had two spear-throwers and two spears now, her own and Zarbo's.

"I'll never do it right!" said Fidday after several tries.

"That's what I used to say. But you will!"

Fidday kept trying, and on the second day she was throwing the spear a short distance.

"You're learning fast!" said Malu.

And Malu learned something, too, standing with Fidday at the throwing line, watching their spears soar.

"Throwing spear *with* someone is nice," Malu said. "I always had to do it alone."

They threw spear every day the hunters were gone. While they were practicing, Malu's worries were just a nibble at the back of her mind.

\* \* \*

The sixth day of waiting droned on slowly. Strands of fear twisted through Malu's hopes that all was well. The mammoths were so enormous, so powerful. There might be an accident, or an avalanche—so many things could go wrong.

In the afternoon, one by one, the women and girls

left the hearth to look out over the snowy valley. At last . . .

"They're coming! They're coming!" The cries were joyful. That meant no one was missing! Soon the hunters, with great humps of meat on their backs, entered with loud *Ho-las*. They must have found the mammoths! But no. They carried no tusks.

While she was searching for Father's face, her eyes met Gunto's, and instantly they both looked away.

"We tracked a few stray bison—carried all we could!" Father smiled broadly.

Bison was great meat, second only to mammoth— haunches, fleshy sides of ribs, forelegs, organs. The warm, hairy hides to cover doorways and roof summer huts. Even tails and heads with their short curved horns, for Sosho's medicines and healing potions.

Maybe bison meant that the Animal Master was feeling more favorable toward them now. Maybe mammoths next time.

They celebrated with a great feast. The Clan Hall was quiet except for the fire snapping, and sounds of chewing and gulping, as people tore into their chunks of meat with their teeth. Malu stopped eating—warm and full at last.

There was enough for more feasts, for several nights. The hunters made plans to make another long search, after these days of rest and hearty eating.

"We'll make as many searches as it takes to find those mammoths!" said Olik.

Ardap sat smoothing his fingers over a new flute he'd made from the leg bone of a deer, Zarbo watching at his side. If there was going to be music, Malu wanted to hear it. With Kono, she sat beside them.

Ardap held up the flute, squinting at the holes he'd drilled in it.

"Come on, let's hear it!" said Zarbo.

Ardap put it to his lips, stopped some of the holes with his fingers, and blew a few notes, so clear and high Malu clapped her hands with delight. He smiled and blew on.

A hunter picked up his goat horn, tilting the wide end toward the ceiling. The deeper tones, blending with the singing flute, filled Malu's head. She lay back, resting her head on Kono's back.

The glow of the firelight blurred through Malu's half-lowered eyelashes. The rhythm of the music became one with the in and out of her breathing. She wanted to feel like this forever.

Something across the hearth drew her gaze. Gunto's eyes were fixed on her. Blinking, he looked hastily away. But the spell of the evening was broken.

She sat up. Zarbo was half-asleep, but Ardap was still blowing on his flute, a sad, haunting tune.

The fire was low. It was late. She must take Kono for their nightly walk to the pine grove before going to her sleeping shelf.

Outside on the Great Ledge, the air was freezing. She ran with Kono to the family cave for warmer clothing. Then they ran back, past the Clan Hall, and started down the hillside path.

Malu stopped. She thought she heard something as she stepped onto the path. Footsteps? She turned. Must have been her imagination, or Kono wouldn't be tugging at the strap, padding on down the hill.

Something snapped—like a twig being stepped on. Kono looked over her shoulder, stood still a moment, and walked on. If Kono wasn't alarmed, she shouldn't be. At the bottom of the hill they followed the path that led through a clearing and on into the pine grove.

In the clearing she stopped to look up to the cliff. The Clan Hall entrance was almost straight overhead. In winter, when trees were bare of leaves, she could see how close it really was. So near, so near.

The face of cliff gleamed white in the moonlight. The Clan Hall entrance, with its wide, arching rock overhanging it, looked like a smiling mouth. When a cloud scudded across the moon, the cliff briefly darkened.

Someone—a dark shape—moved across the mouth. *Who was up there?* She laughed at herself. It could be anybody, maybe one of her friends going home. The shape moved along the ledge. Then she saw nothing. There was a tiny rolling sound—like a stone dislodged, falling down the cliff.

Kono growled, deep and rumbling. *Who was up there?* Kono stiffened and growled louder. Malu strained to hear—nothing. Kono snarled and lunged. Malu braced her feet and held the strap tight.

*Hoo!* Something grazed her shoulder. She fell. Just beyond her, a loud thud—a thud she knew well: a spear, falling flat on the ground.

Who? What? *Where was Kono?* The strap had pulled off her wrist.

"Kono! Kono!" she screamed. "Come back, Kono!"

Malu ran. Not the path—too long. Up the cliff. Kono! Where was she? Climb, climb faster! No breath left to call her.

At the top—too late. Screams and shrieks from the Clan Hall.

Malu was shaking all over. Her breath, short stabs of pain. Running inside, she heard Kono snarling—a fierce snarling she'd never heard before.

She pushed through the crowd. Gunto, lying on the floor, blood running from his arm, eyes wide with shock. Kono, standing over him, bristling, fangs bared. Father and Ardap yanking Kono's strap.

She darted over, calling "Come!" and Kono leaped to her side.

Sosho rushing to Gunto, reaching into his medicine sack.

"Hurry! He'll bleed his life out!" Gunto's mother shouted. She glared at Malu. "Hasn't enough happened to him without this!"

Malu and Father took Kono to the entrance. Malu crouched over her, stroking her back to calm her.

"You've got her now?" Father's eyes were dark and accusing. When she nodded, he said, "I have to see how Gunto is."

She hoped Gunto was all right . . . but all she could think of was Kono. Kono was doomed.

She cried into Kono's ruff. "You're so good, Kono! We tried so hard, and you did everything right. This shouldn't have happened!"

"Malu." It was Mother. "Gunto is going to be all right. It was a flesh wound, a lot of bleeding, that's all. Lucky that Ardap ran and grabbed Kono's strap right away."

A shout rang out. Gunto. The shock had worn off. "Wolf bite! The wolf bit me! Kill the wolf!"

"Kill the wolf! Kill the wolf!" One voice, then other voices taking up the cry.

Sosho raised his hand for silence. "The wolf harmed one of the people. The vow is broken. The wolf will die."

Malu stared through her tears. Father was beside her, his eyes sad now.

"My wolf, my Kono!" Malu cried.

"I'm getting my spear! I'll kill that wolf right now!" said Gunto's father.

Sosho held up his hand. "We will not dishonor the Moon Goddess. The proper rites will be observed. By her decree, the killing will take place at dawn."

Save Kono. *Do* something! Malu brushed her sleeve across her eyes. Wait! No one knew *why* Kono bit

Gunto. Malu pressed Kono's strap into Father's hand and ran forward.

"I am sorry, Gunto. I hope your wound heals fast. It is a great wrong that my wolf bit you."

"You *should* be sorry!"

She took a deep breath. "I've done everything I could to keep the vow—to keep Kono from harming anyone. But Kono was only trying to protect me, because your spear struck me, Gunto."

"You—you're lying," said Gunto.

There was a murmur from the crowd. Mother moved to her side. "Malu does not lie."

Malu's voice shook. "Gunto *did* throw his spear. I was taking Kono to the pine grove. He stood below the ledge and threw it. It wasn't a direct hit. It grazed my shoulder and made me fall down."

Gunto looked around the crowd and sneered. "It wouldn't make any sense for me to throw a spear at you!"

Malu's voice stopped shaking. "But your spear *did* hit me, and Kono was only trying to protect me when she bit you. Didn't you run in here just ahead of Kono?"

Some people nodded.

"People are always coming and going," Gunto said.

"Never mind. I know you weren't trying to hit me. You were trying to hit *Kono!* But you didn't aim right!"

"I did, too!" Gunto gasped. "I—I mean, I would have aimed right, *if* I threw it, but I *didn't!*"

His own words. Malu closed her eyes. Surely Sosho must spare Kono now.

103

Sosho broke the silence. "Where is your spear now, Gunto?"

Gunto looked around as if he might see it.

Malu said, "I heard it land after it struck me. I *know* the sound of a spear that lands flat! The spear is at the edge of the clearing."

"Gunto, can you show us your spear?" Sosho asked.

"I can't remember exactly where I left it. Somewhere around here, I think."

"Malu, can you show us where the spear struck you?" Sosho asked.

"Maybe it doesn't show." Her fingers felt her shoulder. She pointed to a small tear in the leather. "The spear must have nicked it here when it flew by."

Sosho looked at it, his face grim. He sent three hunters to look for the spear.

Hope came to her then. She went back to Kono and sat by her, patting her back and silently praying to the Moon Goddess.

Sosho walked out to the Great Ledge, motioning that no one should follow. The clan waited. Once Gunto started to say Malu's name, but when people stared at him, hard-eyed, he shut his mouth.

The three hunters returned with Sosho. As people made way for them, everyone's eyes were on the spear.

"This was found at the edge of the clearing. Gunto, isn't this your spear?"

"It looks like it."

"*Is* it your spear?" Sosho's face was icily distant.

"Yes."

"Hear this now. We are faced with broken vows. The wolf under Malu's care has harmed one of the people, breaking the vow of the Moon Goddess. And Gunto has broken his vows as a hunter. These we have all seen with our eyes and heard with our ears. As is proper, the wolf's killing rites will be at dawn tomorrow."

Killing rites! Malu put her hands over her face. Kono! She *was* losing Kono!

Sosho went on speaking. "Then all members of the hunting band will go to the Magic Chamber to determine Gunto's fate."

Sosho came to Malu. His voice was gentle. "What is meant to be will be. I can do many things, but I cannot change consequences, my child."

Malu leaned over Kono and clung to her.

Mother's arms went around her. "Come home with me, Malu."

Kono looked at Malu, her golden eyes questioning. Walking along the ledge, Kono pressed her head against Malu's side and whined. Kono didn't know why Malu was sad, but she sensed Malu's pain.

"Tether Kono's strap to the rock, Malu," said Father. Malu nodded. Then she dropped to Kono's side and sobbed. Mother laid Malu's bearskin over Malu and her wolf.

"I wish I could take away your pain," said Mother.

Father touched her shoulder. "I, too." He and Mother

went to their sleeping shelf, around a turn in the cave wall.

The fire shed a dim orange glow. The damp wood sputtered and snapped. Malu snuffled into Kono's fur. Kono whined.

It hurt too much! She cried out, "Kono, my wolf! I can't live without you!"

"Malu," Father called softly, "I want you to know, it will—it will be very quick. Kono will not suffer."

"But she will! She already knows something terrible is happening!"

There was a long silence from their sleeping shelf.

"We shall endure," said Mother.

"We shall endure," Father repeated.

Malu took a deep breath. "We shall endure," she whispered. But could she endure this?

She must stay awake all night—to share this last night with Kono. She wrapped her arms around the wolf and looked at the hearth.

The fire burned low. She stopped sobbing. Kono napped and awoke, napped and awoke. Malu turned over, turned back, wept some more, and shifted around again. How long the night was—and how short.

She kicked out of the bearskin. She'd look at the moon with Kono. Maybe, *maybe* there would be a magical answer in the sky, the Moon Goddess speaking in the voices of the wolves.

The moon was low in the sky. She sat on the ledge, leaning against the cliff, Kono snuggled against her.

She rubbed Kono's chest, waiting, listening for the wolves, looking into the sky.

But tonight there was no magic in the moon, no wolfsong—only a cold breeze, and falling snow that dimmed the moon.

What would Kono do if *Malu* were the one to be killed? Kono would do anything—*anything!*—to save her. How could *she* do less for Kono?

She looked across the treetops to the valley, white with snow. Beyond was the river, and, still farther, all that great empty space. She'd go there—far away, where no one could find them.

Yes! They'd find a little cave to live in. She'd take everything she needed to live with and hunt with. And she would fear nothing, with Kono to protect her.

"We can do it!" she whispered. "You will live, Kono."

But—leave Mother and Father? Sosho, Zarbo, and Ardap? Fidday, Talva, and Varda? Her clan, the Clan of the Cliff? Leave them all, forever?

There was really no choice. She looked at the pale moon. Kono was watching the moon, too. If they didn't go, Kono would never see another night's moon.

*Yes.* She must hurry.

# CHAPTER EIGHT

The clicking of Kono's claws on the rock floor of the cave sounded so loud she thought Mother and Father would surely waken. She stopped Kono, and listened. Only silence.

She spread out her sleeping skin near the front of the cave. How heavy the bearskin was! To carry it on her back with her other gear . . . she had to, that was all—or she'd freeze.

What should she take? If only she had time to think! The moon was low in the sky—already half the night was gone, and by dawn she and Kono must be far away.

Food, of course. A few strips of dried meat from the keeping shelf, to last until she could take time to hunt. A basket, a small clay vessel. Her fire-starting stone and stick, and some dry tinder. Straps and thongs.

Kono watched every move Malu made, standing up

whenever Malu went near the entrance. "You're coming with me—don't worry," Malu wanted to say, but she didn't dare even to whisper.

A memory flashed—Sosho putting dried moss on Zarbo's wounded leg. Just in case, she'd take some moss. There'd be no Sosho, no Mother and Father to care for her.

She blinked her eyes fast. Mustn't think about that now.

She felt under her sleeping shelf for her belongings. Her two spears she stood at the entrance. The rest she piled on her bearskin—her knives, ax, slingshot, bag of stones—a spear-thrower. Which one, the wolf or the horse? Zarbo's horse was beautiful, but she had practiced so long with her own, that was the one she'd take.

She shook her head. Mustn't think of Zarbo now, either.

Reaching farther under her sleeping shelf, she pulled out her treasure sack—the strip of hide with Kono's baby tooth, the sparkly stone, the wooden fish—all things she loved. She hugged it a moment, longing to take it—but no. Too much to carry.

She stuffed part of the pile into a sack and rolled the rest inside the bearskin, lashing it tight. She tied thongs around her waist to hang her tools and gear on. She slung the bearskin onto her back—so heavy!—added the sack, and reached for her spears. She must go now. But—

Mother and Father! If only she could touch them and say good-bye. She tiptoed to the back of the cave, feeling for the bend in the wall, and beyond toward their sleeping shelf. She saw nothing in the dark, but she heard their breathing. She put out her hand—no!

She didn't *want* to leave them. If only she could *tell* them so! But how? Her treasure sack! She put Zarbo's spear-thrower in it, too, and set it by their sleeping shelf. They'd know it was a sign from her.

She tiptoed to the entrance and, with a spear in each hand, pushed through the doorskin flap with Kono. No turning back now. She stood on the ledge a moment, pulling her fur hood snug. The moon was a faint blur through the whirling snowflakes.

She started walking to the hillside path. All those small caves where people were sleeping—she had to pass by them—and go by the Clan Hall, too. What if someone was awake and saw her? Trembling, she turned down the path.

She would head for the river. The heavy load on her back was hard to balance as she walked down the hillside path, made slick by the falling snow. But she was grateful for the snow, for it would hide her tracks. At the bottom she looked back at the cliff, shuddering, but this time no one was up there.

Here, where the land sloped gently down toward the river, she could walk fast. She slipped the strap off Kono to let her run free. Which way should she go when she reached the river? Where could she find a safe place to live? A small cave, near flowing water—far away from the clan, so they'd never find her, even by chance while hunting.

First, she decided, she'd cross the river. Crossing on ice was treacherous even in daylight. No one would imagine she'd pick the hardest way to go.

Reaching the river, she walked downstream, away from the thunder of the waterfall. Beyond the river bend where the water was calm, the ice should be solid—as solid as river ice ever was over such swirling, tumbling waters.

With Kono frisking ahead, she walked fast along the bank. Moonlight was already fading. As she reached the bend, darkness lay thick about her. Walk across ice she couldn't even see? Was she foolish? Should she turn back?

Kono leaped and put her paws on Malu's shoulders.

"You're telling me to go ahead, aren't you?" Malu said. She jabbed a spear into the ground. "We must!"

Kono ran onto the ice and disappeared. Malu stood at the edge, hearing water gurgle below. Imagine falling through it! Go. Don't stand there. She took her first step, balancing with a spear in each hand.

Mustn't step on thin ice. But in the dark, how could she tell where it was thin? She stretched out a foot, pressing with her heel. The ice didn't crack. She took another step, leaning on her spears, and reached out again with her other foot.

But this was no good! Until she *stood* on the ice, she couldn't be sure it wouldn't break.

The next step might be disaster. She couldn't move. Kono ran a circle around her—so light on those four quick feet—and then she ran off, out of sight. Malu had never felt so alone.

"Come, Kono!" she called. The wolf leaped and knocked into one of the spears. As Malu tightened her grip, the shaft end struck the ice hard—*thunk!*

That thud—she *knew* thin ice wouldn't make a solid sound like that. "Ho-la!" she cried. Just listen to the ice! Rap the spear on it before each step. She rapped, listened for a thud, and stepped forward. Safe. She kept on rapping and stepping with the thuds.

*Tap!* Thin ice. Rap ice at her side—shuffle that way—rap for a thud. She was getting closer to the opposite bank.

Rap the spear. No rap! Nothing! She flung herself backward as the river sucked the spear from her hand. She sat gasping. One spear gone!

When she could stand up, she slowly swept the end of the other spear across the spot ahead. There was a hole in the ice there, perhaps a breathing hole for river animals.

She sidestepped, and heard a *thunk*. As she rapped and walked, the bank loomed close, faintly white in the dark. Near the edge, the ice gave back tapping sounds. There was thin ice all along this bank. The wolf leaped across, but Malu couldn't jump that far.

Her only chance was to try vaulting across with the spear.

She backed up, ran, lifted on the spear, and crashed onto the bank. Kono greeted her with a face-licking.

"We did it!" Laughing, half-crying with relief, Malu pushed at Kono. "Let me up!"

Now, where to go? The hunters hardly ever went up the north mountains, saying it was poor for hunting. Their hunting grounds were the mountains east of the caves, for goats, and southeast for mammoths, where they used to graze. Westward lay the clan's summer grounds. Yes, she must go north.

She turned upriver, walking easily on the smooth flat bank. She fancied she could see, far across the other side, the cliff of the caves. Mother and Father would soon awaken and find her gone. She brushed her wrist across her damp eyes.

Darkness was already fading. She'd soon be visible if an early riser came down to the river. She walked faster, looking for a way to climb up the cliff, which was higher and steeper than she remembered.

She saw the two big trees where the flint mine was, and the coil of rope hung on a branch. She'd walked here with Father and Olik when she was little, and sat on the mound of stones and dirt, watching as they slid down the rope to the bottom of the shaft. All the hunters came here for the flint that they could flake off into strong, sharp edges for their blades and spear-points.

How simple her life had been then, skipping along, holding Father's hand. And now she was fleeing from her family and clan.

She must find a path or an easier slope to climb, so she could head away from the river. Kono made little runs to sniff, roll in the snow, trot back to her, and run ahead again. Now that it was light enough to see where Kono was, she felt less alone.

Kono drank from a pool of water ahead, where a stream cascaded down the cliff. Pulling off her mitts, Malu cupped her hands into the icy water. It tasted good, but it wasn't the warm broth Mother gave her each morning to sip by the fire. Her eyes teared. Mustn't think of Mother now. She took out two strips of dried meat.

"One for you and one for me," she said to Kono. Malu chewed the sticklike meat until her mouth juices warmed it and drew out the meat taste. She wanted more, but she must make the meat last.

Tracing the stream upward with her eyes, she saw that the cliff was less steep here. She lashed her spear to her bundle and climbed, grabbing branches when she lost her footing. Kono leaped and scratched her way up. By the time the sun rose, the river was out of sight below, and soon the cliff crested into a gentle slope. At last! She could walk now.

She was tired. She leaned on the spear and thought of Zarbo with his forked stick. Oh, Zarbo! He would understand why she had gone.

The stream was shallow here, crusted with ice. Trees and bushes stood like black skeletons against the snow. A few more snowflakes fell, and then stopped.

They kept following the stream. Not until the sun was high did she stop to drink and eat again. The bright sun made her eyes feel too heavy to keep open. Her head snapped up—she had dozed. She must stay awake!

She started walking again. Though the ground was level, she stumbled again and again over rocks and roots hidden under the snow. She floundered along, worrying about finding a shelter from the cold and from the animals that roamed by night. How much longer could she drag herself on?

Suddenly Kono took off, running in a zigzag chase after something small and white against the snow—a hare dodging to escape. Fresh meat!

Malu flung down the spear, yanked loose from her burdens, and set a stone in her slingshot as she ran. She aimed, shot—and missed. Kono chased the hare until it disappeared. The wolf dug furiously into a snowbank, but the hare was gone.

Malu squinted at the snow, now glittering in the afternoon sun. She was dead-tired, she had lost a spear, and she had missed that hare. What would happen to her and Kono?

Kono! Where had she gone after chasing the hare?

Screaming, "Kono, Kono!" she ran until she spotted her wolf near a sharp rise. She called, but Kono didn't come. Malu numbly plodded toward her and saw that Kono was standing at an opening to . . . What was it? A cave!

The way the cave faced away from the stream, Malu would have missed seeing it. She almost rushed inside, but knew better. A cave bear or lion might live here. She looped the strap over the wolf's head and looked for tracks. But the only footprints were their own.

With great snorting sniffs, Kono led the way in. It was a small cave, higher than it was wide. A streak of sunlight slanted in, showing a clean rubble of stones, and no trace of animal life. At the back was another opening, wide but short. Since she'd have to bend over to enter it—and anyway, Kono had stopped sniffing— the cave must be safe.

"We'll have a place to sleep tonight, Kono!" said Malu, laying down her sack and bearskin. Fire came first. She went out to gather wood. The snow lay lightly upon the brush and fallen branches. With her ax she broke the longer pieces. She carried in many loads, enough to last the night.

Making a tiny hill of tinder on her fire-making stone, she held the twirling stick upright between the palms of her hands, resting the end on her stone by the tinder. She rubbed her palms together fast, back and forth, pushing down, and still twirling, letting her palms rise to the top of the stick—faster and faster she twirled it.

A wisp of smoke arose. She twirled still faster, and

a spark flickered. She blew on it gently, making more smoke plume upward, and a tiny flame burst out. Taking care not to smother it, she laid twigs across it.

Soon a blazing fire warmed her and brightened the cave. She brought water from the stream in her clay vessel and stood it in the fire. She added a bit of the fat she had brought along, and to melt it, stirred it with a twig.

From the small roll of deerskin that held the dried meat, she took the last pieces out. Saying, "Two for you, two for me, and four for tomorrow," she sat by the fire, chewing and drinking.

The fat-flavored water wasn't much like Mother's bone broth, but as she drank it, she felt warm inside and out. Kono laid her head on her paws, leaning into Malu.

They were snug and warm here in their little cave. Tomorrow they would hunt. They'd eat fresh meat. They'd start out again, looking for a place to live— far, far away.

*   *   *

She wakened to gray shadows. Where was the meaty fragrance from Mother's steaming bone broth?

Oh, no. She was far from home, lying on the floor of a strange cave. Everything was strange—nothing familiar except what she had brought with her. Kono raised her head and yawned.

"Kono—I have you!" Malu pressed her head into Kono's neck. But she didn't have Mother and Father. Suddenly sobs choked her.

"Mother! Father!" she cried, and wiped her eyes. They would have seen her empty sleeping shelf by now. How they must be suffering! Why did saving Kono have to mean hurting them?

Kono whined sympathetically. Malu patted Kono's head and threw back the bearskin.

"We'll go hunting, Kono. Maybe we'll get that hare—or something even better. I'll make broth every morning, too."

The fire had died down to a few embers. Shivering, Malu blew on them and added sticks. As an orange glow slowly spread across the walls of the cave, Malu took out the last four pieces of dried meat, looking at them hungrily. Should they each have one now, saving two for later, in case they found no game?

No. Hunters needed food. She threw Kono two pieces and, one after the other, stuffed the other two in her mouth. Still chewing on the stiff, dry meat, Malu pulled the hood of her shirt tight about her face, and walked outside.

The sky, though cloudy, was bright. The wind had stopped, but left its traces in snow that piled lopsidedly on rocks and curved in shallow sweeps around tree trunks and bushes.

But that wasn't what she had hoped to see in the snow: animal footprints. She heard no bird calls. The air was so clear and empty, an eerie feeling prickled through her.

The hunters had said this place had little game. Was there no life here but that hare that got away? The Animal Master! She would have to try talking to him.

"Animal Master, I pray for forgiveness if I have offended you. I did not mean to. My wolf and I have had no fresh meat for two days. Our dried meat is gone. I pray that you will send us game."

Would that win his favor? "Ho-la!" she said loudly, to show him—if he listened to her—that she had faith in his kindness.

Kono raced up the opposite slope and back, hitting Malu broadside with a body slam. Malu fell, laughing, and pulled Kono down on top of her. They rolled around in the snow, Kono pretending to bite and growl. Malu pushed Kono's nose into the snow and held it there until Kono pulled loose, yipping wildly, running circles around her.

Suddenly feeling better, Malu ran back to the cave for her hunting gear—spear-thrower hung from her shoulder, and slingshot, bag of stones, knife, and ax tied to her waist thong. Spear in hand, she touched her finger to the flint point. She knew every flake she had chipped to form it. It was sharp—sharp enough, she hoped, to pierce any animal's tough hide. With luck, she would prove it soon.

Malu and Kono leaped across the stream and began walking up the slope. No tracks or scat here, either, and not a mark on the snow. She thought again about the Animal Master. Maybe he had to see if she, a girl, was worthy. She'd show him she was a real hunter by hunting all day, if that was what she had to do.

As she walked, Kono frisked back and forth, tunneling her nose under the snow, sniffing and snorting. When Kono raised her head, a silly puff of white topped her black nose.

After changing directions several times, Malu reached the top of the slope. To check her bearings, she looked back down at the stream and the cave.

A small scuffling sound made her look around. A wriggling mouse dangled by its tail from Kono's mouth. With a flip of her head, Kono tossed the mouse in the air, caught it in her open jaws, and ate it.

Malu kept watching. Kono stood still, head cocked. Suddenly she sprang straight up in the air and in one flowing motion landed, her four feet close together. She pushed her muzzle between her paws and snatched up the mouse she had caught. A toss of the mouse, a snap of her jaws—and the second mouse was gone.

"Good wolf!" said Malu. She sat down in the snow to watch Kono's joyful frenzy of leaping, snapping, and gulping.

Kono had found a big mouse clan. Malu's belly pinched with hunger, but she wanted Kono to eat her fill. When Kono sat licking her chops, Malu took a few steps, wondering which way to go now.

Kono trotted ahead and suddenly stopped to stare up the slope, her ears perked to attention. Malu saw no prey, but, trusting Kono's nose, she fitted a stone into her slingshot and waited.

She spied a movement—bird's feet scratching in the snow—a ptarmigan in its white winter feathers. Telling Kono to stay, Malu shot the stone.

With a weak flap of its wings, the bird fell back and lay still. Malu and Kono ran up the slope.

But something white and furry darted out of the bushes and pounced on the ptarmigan—a fox—and it was taking her bird! Kono growled and dashed after the fox. Malu fitted another stone into the sling as she ran.

Dragging the ptarmigan by the neck, the fox looked back and saw Kono leaping toward it in great bounds. The fox dropped the bird and fled, and Kono kept chasing it as Malu picked up the ptarmigan.

She called Kono. Kono seemed more interested in chasing the fox, but she loped back and sniffed the bird. Malu slit open the belly and let the guts fall for Kono to eat. After scrubbing the body cavity with handfuls of snow, Malu hung the carcass by the legs from her waist thong.

She longed to run back to the cave and cook the bird right away. But she mustn't stop now. Tomorrow the Animal Master might be less generous.

Almost groaning with hunger, Malu kept walking and looking. Kono ran around with her nose to the ground, but no scent or sound made her ears perk up. After a full day's hunt, they had only the ptarmigan—large for a ptarmigan, but still just small game. All this way, she had carried around her spear and thrower and had yet to see an animal big enough to spear.

Would there be any game tomorrow? They shouldn't have eaten all their dried meat. Kono wouldn't starve, with all those mice—but what about her?

They started back to the cave. Kono stopped by a big tree ahead. With her hackles high, ears pointed forward close to her head, she sniffed all around it. She looked at Malu and growled low.

Malu saw long, deep scratches in the bark. A bear taller than a man had marked these grounds as its own, but the dried sap in the scratches meant the bear hadn't been here recently. Malu swept snow off a patch of ground by the tree, and saw paw prints made in mud before the ground froze. What big feet! Bigger than her two mitted hands together, she saw when she set them into a paw print.

This bear was probably deep asleep. But Malu knew that during its winter sleep, a cave bear could waken at any time, roaring its hunger and meanness. The hunters said that no animal was as savage as a cave bear in winter.

That opening at the back of their cave! What if it was the bear's cave, and the bear was sleeping back there? And what if its hunger would make the bear waken?

It could be dangerous to stay here. But it was the only cave they'd seen all yesterday, and already long purple shadows stretched across the snow. They *had* to sleep here tonight. She'd build a bigger fire and keep it blazing all night.

Kono's waving tail and bounding leaps cheered Malu as she gathered wood for the fire. After plucking the ptarmigan's feathers, she set it over the flames, and went back to gather armloads of branches and brush in the fast-fading light. Each time, before going out again, she poked at the roasting ptarmigan to see if it was done. Not yet—not yet. When it was too dark to see, she stayed inside, hoping the pile of wood would keep the fire ablaze all night.

A rich aroma arose—ah! She touched a leg of the bird. It moved freely. Fresh-roasted meat! She gave some breast meat to Kono and picked up the whole ptarmigan to chew on. So good! She gave more meat to Kono and nibbled the last scraps off the legs and wings.

After two lean days, this was a feast! She licked her fingers, leaned back, and yawned. She hadn't thought of the bear since starting to eat. The jagged edge of fear was gone, but not the worry.

She set down the sleeping skin so that the fire would be between her and the cave's back opening. Putting her arm around Kono, she tried to sleep, but when her eyes shut, a big bear shape prowled in her mind. She couldn't sleep with the terrible unknowing.

She mustn't let the fire burn low. It was a long night of feeding the fire and waiting for morning's light when they'd set out. Somewhere out there they'd find a cave of their own.

# CHAPTER NINE

A thin strip of light slanted into the cave. Daylight, at last. She'd fallen asleep after being awake most of the night. She sprang out of the bearskin, quickly bundling up her belongings, after taking the spear-thrower out of the sack she carried on her back. One fear that had struck her during the night was that the cave bear would charge at her, and she wouldn't be able to get at her spear-thrower fast enough. There were enough risks she *had* to take, without that.

Kono sat by the entrance, watching her tighten the straps across her back. With the spear-thrower hung on a shoulder thong, and the slingshot at her waist, she took her spear in hand and left the cave.

She walked fast, crossing the stream and following it up the slope where they'd hunted yesterday. Kono growled as they passed the cave bear's scratching tree.

They walked beyond the spot where she'd killed

the ptarmigan. The slope went up and up endlessly, and the snow here had frozen into an icy crust. Each step was a struggle to keep from sliding backward. Even Kono was slipping, and pawing madly to gain her footing.

"Come, Kono, let's go *across* the hill," Malu said, panting. The curve of the slope here was right—it would take them north and east.

She had to rest. Fear of the cave bear had quickened her, but now she could hardly make herself move. She longed to lie down. No—mustn't think about sleep. Keep walking! She scanned the snow for animal tracks, but saw none. Her hopes of finding food faded.

Kono found more mice. Malu sat on a fallen log to let her eat her fill. One mouse and then another and another—the little animals added up to a bellyful of meat for a wolf. As Kono licked her chops, Malu felt hungrier than before.

The bundles on her back grew heavier. Her feet dragged. Even one strip of tough dried meat—if she only had it now.

When Kono drank from the stream, Malu cupped her hands and drank, too, until her fingers were so frozen she couldn't keep them cupped.

Hunching her load higher on her back, she followed Kono, who now was loping ahead and nosing around. At a rocky rise of the land, a streamlet cascaded down, leaving long frozen streamers. Malu broke off a long icicle to suck on.

Suddenly Kono sprang into long running leaps, chasing a hare. A vision of meat roasting over a fire made Malu run, but her pounding feet broke through the ice crust into the soft snow beneath. She put a stone in the slingshot and kept clumping along anyway, for the hare in its zigzagging flight might double back.

Kono caught the hare and snapped its neck. Picking it up, she looked at Malu and loped back to her, the hare swinging from her mouth. She dropped it at Malu's feet and nudged Malu's arm with her head. A picture flicked into Malu's mind—Gray Wolf bringing meat to Old Wolf.

"Oh, Kono," she said, "I used to feed you. Now you're feeding me." She swallowed hard. Sensing it was the proper wolf thing to do, she gazed into Kono's golden eyes.

She picked up the hare and gutted it—a morsel for Kono. She shouldn't stop to eat until they found a shelter for the night. But just ahead, alongside a boulder, was a flat rock for a hearth, and beyond, scattered dead tree limbs for a fire. Anyway, shouldn't she show Kono her appreciation by eating the hare immediately?

She made fire, skinned the hare, and, for quick roasting, cut it in pieces. She sat in the lee of the boulder, yawning and looking around. The smell was tantalizing, and at last it was done. She ripped strips of meat off the bones with her teeth. She rolled it on her tongue and chewed, closing her eyes to prolong the taste and feel of it. She packed the scraps and bones in her meat sack. The pelt she left on the rock. She hated to, but she mustn't carry one more thing.

Kono made a leap at the pelt. She chewed it, rolled on it, tossed it high, and chased it. She caught it and shook it ferociously. It flapped—*snap, snap*—around her ears.

Kono looked so funny Malu snatched at the pelt and tugged. Kono growled and pulled back. Malu got a better grip, and they slid around, pulling each other back and forth until Kono sat back on her haunches and yanked the pelt from her hand. Malu lay in the snow laughing, while Kono ran circles around her.

This was how they had played at home. She sighed. "Come, Kono. Let's go."

The breeze was stronger. A cloud shadow swept across them and flitted up the slope. The winter sun was already lowering in the sky behind them.

"Soon we'll find a cave, I just know it!" Malu said.

As the slope became steeper, the meat, so warm and solid inside her, lent strength to her legs. The breeze gusted up into an icy wind, and she pulled her hood tight across her forehead.

A flock of small birds twittered in some bushes ahead. With a stone ready in her sling, Malu crept closer, Kono stalking silently beside her. Malu shot one, then another, before the flock startled and flew off. Small, these birds, but meat all the same. She swooped them up and tucked them in her meat sack.

Ahead, the slope ended in a sharp line against the sky. What lay beyond? Climbing faster, she found herself at a jagged crest, looking down a cliff. The wind howled, and the trees clinging to the cliff swayed and creaked. Turning her back to the wind, Malu huddled tight into herself.

Here at the top, the snow was mostly blown away, and she could walk more easily as she looked for a way down. A sudden blast of wind-driven snow nearly blew her off balance.

She blinked her eyes fast to keep Kono in sight. The wolf was running around in circles, burrowing her nose in the snow and lightheartedly leaping and pouncing—catching mice again.

Wolves' lives were certainly easier than people's. *She* had to plan and worry, but not Kono.

She stirred herself. Daylight was already dimming. She couldn't stay up *here*. Yet in the howling wind and with her top-heavy load, she couldn't risk picking her way down among the snow-covered rocks. Just then the fickle wind let up.

"Go, Kono, down here!" she called. Kono came and led the way. Malu stepped down into the snow, skidding, and grabbing bushes and trees. Then Kono found a narrow zigzagging path, probably made by animals going to drink from a stream below.

She kept looking through the swirling snow for caves. She must find one soon, for in a gorge, darkness would come fast. At every shadowed rock or overhang, boulder or bush, she stopped to look. But there were no caves, just clefts open to the sky. She felt a catch in her throat. Would they have to sleep in the open, on this terrible night?

Behind a rockfall she saw an opening barely tall enough to enter, if she stooped. It was more like a hole than a cave, hardly wider than it was high. The two of them, she and Kono, could lie down in it, but there was no space for a fire, and they *must* have a fire.

She shook her head and walked on. She could hardly see, and soon the only light would be from the pale, thin moon, now rising over the cliff.

Malu shivered and turned back. That hole would have to be their shelter. In the space between the shelter and the rocks in front of it, she could build a fire. It wouldn't warm them much, but it would keep away animals.

"This isn't even a real cave, Kono," she said, "but one good thing—no animal can be hiding in it."

She gathered wood, made fire, and set up for the night, arranging the knife and spear beside her on the sleeping skin. She hung the two bird carcasses from a tree root that poked through the side of the shelter.

She lay down and tugged the sleeping skin over them both. Even with the stop to eat the hare, they had come far today, and the falling snow would keep their whereabouts secret. She felt safe, hidden here, with the fire burning and Kono beside her. She could sleep tonight.

She looked out at the stars in the patch of dark sky above the rocks. There was the big star, sparkling at her—the one she always looked for back home, because of Father's story. When she was little, she had never tired of hearing how the Moon Goddess gave the North Star one of the brightest lights of all—next to her own—to guide those who must find their way home at night.

Home. She could never go home. Maybe, right now, Mother and Father were looking at this star. Would they think she was dead? What trouble and sorrow she had brought them!

If only she could send a vision of herself soaring up to that bright star, for them to see that she had food to eat and a shelter to sleep in.

If only she could take Kono home with her! If only, if only. She sobbed into Kono's ruff. Kono held very still as if she knew how Malu felt.

Malu sniffed and looked back at the sky. Mother's and Father's faces! Shimmering in the dark, pale—so pale.

She reached out her arms and sobbed, "Mother! Father!"

But the faces faded away.

\* \* \*

In the morning, Malu could hardly see through her puffy eyelids. She pushed aside the sleeping skin. Why did she have to wake up?

The patch of sky above the rockfall was bright blue. The wind had stopped whistling. The only sound was water gurgling somewhere below. She was right about a stream being here.

Kono stretched, front paws down in front, rear end high, tail waving. Her golden eyes gleamed at Malu. Malu smiled. She remembered the bones in her meat sack and the two little bird carcasses, ready to be cooked. She stirred the embers, piled on branches, and slid the carcasses onto a stick. She'd need water to make broth from the bones.

They went out to relieve themselves. Shivering, Malu pulled down her leggings. Then they ran down the path to the stream. On the far side was a hill with clumps of bushes and scattered trees. Good! They wouldn't have to climb another cliff.

Back at the shelter, Malu made the broth. The birds cooked fast, and Malu sipped the warm broth between bites of meat. How good, this morning meal. She and Kono *would* find a good cave home—farther on—soon.

She loaded up again, and they retraced their steps down to the stream. They jumped from rock to rock to cross it, and walked up the snowy hill beyond.

The only tracks were the footprints they left behind

them. Gradually the hill blended into rolling plains again, with fewer bushes and trees.

Grazing land, here. In summer, herds of bison and aurochs must graze in the high grass, but there was nothing here now. She longed for big game—something to fill her belly—not tiny birds. She walked on faster.

Their long morning shadows marched to the left of them, then shortened and vanished. As they pushed on, their shadows stretched out to the right. Malu's belly pinched. The smooth snow held no promise for hunting.

Where a spring bubbled up, a sheet of water slid over a smooth rock. Malu pressed her mouth to the rock, and drank in small gasps. It was like swallowing icicles. But for a short while her belly felt full.

Kono found more mice. Malu rested, hugging her knees and looking around at the white slopes. When Kono sat back to lick her chops, Malu hunched the bundles higher on her back, and they continued on their way.

Up one rolling slope and down another. Ahead, small birds, pecking dry seedpods—but before Malu could set the stone in her slingshot, they took off in a whirl of wings.

Wings! She should remember to look up at the sky more often. Soaring vultures could lead to a dead animal, and if the carcass was frozen, she and Kono could chase off the vultures and steal some meat.

But the sky was as empty as the land. Up and over one rolling snowy plain after another she plodded.

Grassy plains were not cave country. As the sun sank, Malu looked for *any* kind of shelter. Ahead, finally, she saw a rare outcropping of rock, and laid the bearskin under it. No food since those tiny birds at dawn, but she tried not to think about it. They slept close to the fire under their rock roof.

\* \* \*

The sun in the morning warmed them, but the slopes, blinding white, numbed Malu's vision. She longed for trees, rocks, hills and valleys—anything but this. Every slope they walked up looked like the end of the plains, but when they reached the top, another slope rose ahead.

At last they found a level place. Scrubby bushes pushed up the snow in knobby little mounds, and a few scraggly trees appeared. Still she saw no tracks—no chance of finding food. She didn't want to think how long it was since she'd eaten. Kono had eaten only a few mice, so she must be hungry, too. They walked at a steady pace. There was little to stop for—no food, and for water only the snow she melted in her mouth.

And now she *must* find shelter for the night. It looked hopeless: no caves, no rocks—nothing. At sunset, she turned back to a thicket of thorny bushes that she had passed earlier. Though it had no roof or walls, it was the nearest thing to a shelter she could find.

She pushed her way through the thorny branches and trampled down a flat spot at the center.

"It looks like an old bird's nest," she grumbled to Kono.

She took out her fire stone, twirling stick, and tinder. Kneeling on the branches she had flattened, she felt twigs snapping under her.

Why, these bushes were as dry as the tinder! If she made fire here, everything would be in flames. That meant—sleeping in the open without a fire. She'd never done this, not in all the years of moving between the caves and the summer huts. But she had no choice. Kono would guard her. She rolled out her bearskin.

"This is the worst place we ever stayed in," Malu said. "Stay close to me, Kono."

She slept fitfully, longing for the walls of a cave, or even the rock roof of last night's shelter.

She awoke to hunger pangs again. While relieving herself in the morning, she touched her hand to her belly—a hollow under her ribs. She felt inside her shirt, and her breath whistled out of her. Had her ribs always stuck out like that? She thought of Lone Wolf, wasting away.

"Maybe I'll starve," she said aloud. What was going to happen to her? How much longer could she go without food?

Kono ranged far off, looking for mice. Malu didn't

try to follow. It would waste her strength. She noticed that the slopes ahead were becoming hills, and trees were bigger. There must be water soon. Seeing a clump of trees ahead, a sure sign of water, she walked faster.

Yes! There was a stream here. They drank and kept walking. Where water and trees and bushes were, animals must be, too. In a grove of pine trees she stopped, hearing a scratchy sound overhead. A squirrel on a high branch held a pinecone in its paws, chewing on it to get at the seeds. It dropped the cone and disappeared in the greenery.

That was a good sign. She'd keep going, hoping for game in the still-thicker woods beyond. Kono, who was frisking ahead, suddenly stood still. Malu caught up to her. The wolf was growling a deep rumble—a serious growl.

Malu reached for her spear-thrower. At first she heard nothing. Then a distant crashing sound. Something so big it didn't care if anything heard it, breaking branches, snapping and trampling bushes. Louder and closer. What was it?

Breathing hard, Malu butted her spear shaft against the spear-thrower. She tensed her legs, ready to lunge and throw.

A massive boar charged into the open. Its mean little eyes flashed hot when it saw Kono and Malu. It veered and ran at them, grunting and snorting. With each toss of its head it threatened them with the long tusks that curved up from its lower jaw.

Malu lunged and threw the spear. It struck deep into the boar's shoulder, and the shaft bobbed over it as it roared its fury. But it kept charging!

A horrible truth came to her. With no second spear, she was helpless.

Kono crouched and leaped. Helpless? No. She had Kono.

The boar swiped its tusks at Kono, but she dodged and leaped again, slashing the back of the boar's neck with her fangs. Blood trickled down the boar's side. It thrust its tusks at her again, but Kono darted away, circled behind the boar, and clamped her jaws around its hind leg.

The boar grunted, and Kono hung on. The boar dragged its leg, but was still fighting—twisting and thrusting its tusks as Kono thrashed around, dodging them.

But the boar was slowing down. While Kono was distracting it, Malu ran around to its other side and grabbed the spear shaft. If she could pull it out—

The boar swung its tusks at her leg. Malu barely hopped clear, her hands tugging at the spear. She leaped onto its back as the boar again swung its tusks at her. With a wrenching yank, she freed the spear and fell. Leaping to her feet, she gripped the spear with both hands, raised it high, and put her whole body force into one mighty downward thrust.

The boar staggered. Kono let go of the leg and, leaping toward the head, sank her fangs into the lower neck. Blood spewed out, and the boar's legs collapsed. With a massive shudder, it died.

Malu stood back and stared at the suddenly limp body. All that power and fury—gone. In death, a strong boar and a weak hare were the same.

"That could have been me lying there," she whispered to herself.

Kono walked around the boar, sniffing it.

"Ho-la!" Malu leaped in the air. "We're real hunters! *We* did that!"

She looked again at the carcass. Their search for meat was ended. She saw chunks to roast on a spit, bones to crack for marrow and cook for broth, and hide for sacks and boots. But most of all—more meat than she had ever imagined having.

"We'll never be hungry again, Kono!" she sang out.

First, to butcher it. She could do that. As different as they looked on the outside, animals were much alike on the inside. After all, she had cut up many kinds of animals. The boar was merely bigger.

Knife in hand, she knelt at its side and touched the belly. What tough, hairy hide! She pierced it with the point of the knife and, with both hands gripping the handle, pulled it through the hide, sawing at it, grunting with the effort. With a final slash, the belly opened.

She jerked backward. A big bloody soup of glistening guts bulged out. Big animals *were* like small ones, but this animal—oh, that enormous mass!

Impossible. Just leave it! She turned away.

No, she was a hunter, a hungry hunter. Swallowing hard, she freed the guts from the carcass with a knife, and scooped them all out into the snow, where they lay steaming in the cold air.

Intent now, she knelt by the carcass and felt her way with the knife under the hide, cutting and peeling it back to lay bare a massive haunch. She carved out chunks of flesh, which filled her meat sack. Such a treasure of food! Exulting, she wiped the ax and knife clean in the snow. What a shame to leave all this. But with her heavy gear, this was all she could carry.

Wings flapping. The vultures. She hoisted her belongings onto her back. As the vultures tugged at the pile of guts, they eyed Malu, waiting for her to leave the carcass, knowing that, sooner or later, anything dead was theirs.

As she left with Kono, Malu looked back. The vultures were scrambling over the boar's head, hissing and beating their wings at one another as they fought to peck out the eyes.

She walked fast, urged on by the need to take Kono so far away that they'd never be discovered. But before the sun was high overhead, she realized she was too weak to walk all day without eating, and stopped to make fire. To hasten the cooking, she sliced off thin strips of meat. She could have eaten more, but no matter—it was a feast, even though it was morning and shared by only a girl and a wolf.

By late afternoon they had yet to find a place to stay, and Malu's feet were dragging. She knew she must eat again. As she built another fire, she worried. Were they using up the meat too soon? There was still a lot left, she told herself, enough to keep them going until she could hunt again, and maybe she'd find good hunting soon.

\*   \*   \*

Before dark that night, the best shelter Malu found was a hollow among some boulders. They could sleep by a fire again. She roasted most of the boar meat and returned the little left to her meat sack.

At dawn she awoke in the midst of a dream, in which she was a starving wolf-girl, ripping into the boar carcass with her fangs and eating it raw. She was glad to be just Malu, but the hunger wasn't a dream. She and Kono would share the rest of the boar meat.

As they ate, Malu wondered what to do. She was quite sure she'd gone farther north than the hunters ever went. The land to the east looked more promising than these hills, which seemed to have no caves. She could not wander forever. She must find a cave where they could *stay*—a home.

She called Kono. The wolf leaped at her and put

her paws on Malu's shoulders, panting into her face. Kono's breath reeked of raw mouse, and Malu had to turn away.

They walked straight east. By midday, Malu saw the ground changing to longer, steeper hills, and in the distant haze, blue peaks were faintly outlined against the sky. Tears stung her eyes, making her realize how worried she'd been.

Those high hills—she'd find a cave there! She must get there by tonight. She walked fast. Climbing a hill was harder than walking up slopes, but she liked the pull on her legs. It meant change—and hope.

# CHAPTER TEN

After walking through valleys and climbing many hills, each higher than the other, Malu stood on the brink of a cliff. A cliff, at last! The land broke sharply, falling below in rocky layers. There'd be caves here, she was sure, and with trees growing in a thicket below, water should be flowing there.

Just from standing here, she felt this would be their home. She scrambled down the rocks, with Kono leaping far ahead.

At the bottom—yes, a wide stream running over rocks, rushing so fast that only a fringe of ice had formed. Kono stood in it, lapping noisily. Malu cupped her hands again and again to drink.

On her way down, Malu had noticed several promising breaks in the rock ledges, and now she headed back up for a closer look. One was too big, wide open to the weather. But the next one, by a cleft rock, looked right. Kono sniffed around inside and came out waving her tail.

Malu had to duck her head to go in. She liked the low entrance; it would let in light but shield them from wintry blasts of wind and snow. From the entrance a gentle current of fresh air wafted upward into the darkness of the steep, high ceiling. This cave would not fill with smoke from her fires. She walked around, touching the slanting rock walls. The craggy floor held traces of dirt and pebbles, some rocks, and a scattering of small dried-out bones, none of them fresh.

"A good cave, Kono!" she said. "Big enough, but not too big." She slid the bundles off her back and stretched. Starved as she was, fire always came first. She gathered wood, arranged a circle of stones for a hearth, and soon had a flame going.

Now to find food. The boar meat was gone. She walked along the stream looking for fish—none to be seen. She listened for birdcalls or flapping wings. A raven croaked nearby, and there was a distant answering call—nothing else.

She drank water, and looked around for animal tracks. Not good. She saw only the tiny snow-scratchings of mice.

On the far side of the stream she spotted bigger tracks—but not of game. A wolf had run down to the stream, sinking deeper into the snow where it drank, and then zigzagged back across its own paw prints. Just as Kono would do.

Where was Kono? As Malu walked upstream, a chilling thought came to her. Kono couldn't help but notice other wolves nearby. Then what would she do?

Malu had been able to keep Kono away from the pack at home. Here, where Kono was used to running free, she didn't know what would happen. Kono would obey Malu—if she wanted to. She almost always did, but . . .

Malu found Kono standing on the shallow bank, gobbling down a mouse and quickly pouncing on another one—gorging on mice. Kono looked up momentarily without missing a gulp.

Watching her eat made Malu's hunger pangs worse. She crossed her arms over the pain—no help. Lucky Kono, leaping and catching all those mice.

Food! She longed for any kind of food. Oh, that boar meat she'd had to leave behind!

She hacked at the bank with her ax, hoping to turn over bulbs or roots to cook over the fire. Poking around with her knife, she pulled out a few stringy roots—nothing like the plump ones Mother cooked until they were juicy and tender.

Twigs could be chewed. She had to spit out one that crumbled to dust between her teeth. Another one looked fresh, but it chewed into tough strings of wood. Was there no food here? She sat on a rock, bowing her head on her arms.

"We shall endure." The words whispered in her head. She looked skyward and prayed. "Animal Master, I've had so little meat for so long. I'll gratefully eat anything you send me. Grant me food, I pray."

She watched Kono. After eating many more mice, Kono came to Malu with the tip of a mouse tail dangling from her mouth, like a tiny tongue. The wolf looked so silly that Malu laughed. With a flick of her tongue, Kono swallowed the rest of the tail.

Wolves ate many things people couldn't eat—raw meat, meat stinking with rot, bones, guts and all. And they ate mice—raw mice, of course. She wrinkled her nose, recalling the unpleasant odor on Kono's breath.

But if *she* could catch mice and cook them—why not? She touched her slingshot—mice were too small to shoot. She thought longingly of the small fishing nets on the keeping shelf at home. She'd have to catch them by hand—if she could.

A movement caught her eye. A mouse was creeping under the ice crystals at the edge of the stream. She slapped her hand down on it. Missed. Kono, licking her chops, sat beside her and watched.

Malu took off her mitts and tugged at the wrist thongs to open them wide. She waited—saw another mouse—swooped down with an open mitt. Caught it! She closed the mitt.

Kono kept watching.

"I wish I could catch them like you, Kono." She made a face as a mouse darted under some leaves. She swung the other mitt at it—missed again. But Kono pounced on the mouse, snapped its neck, and dropped it on the ground by Malu.

"Good! Good Kono!" Malu picked up the limp warm body and rubbed Kono's head. "More mice, Kono!"

Kono caught many more, and Malu got another four with her mitt. As she peered around for more, she realized it was almost dark.

Clutching the mittful of dead mice, Malu ran to the cave. She gutted and skinned the mice. Kono licked up the guts. Malu cut off their heads, tails and feet, and set one of the tiny bodies over the fire on a little stick.

It cooked fast. She blew on it and took a tiny bite. It tasted smoky and meaty. Meat at last!

But tiny bones poked at her tongue and gums. They were harder to pick out than fish bones. Hungry as she was, she'd have to eat very slowly. She rolled each piece of meat around with her tongue, feeling for bones before swallowing it.

At last something solid sat in her belly. She wasn't filled—but she wasn't starving. If only mouse-hunting were easier.

After piling wood on the fire, Malu settled into the bearskin with Kono. A good cave, fresh meat, and a fireside for sleeping! Tomorrow they'd find real game. Meat to shoot down with stones—maybe even big game to bring down with her spear.

This cave was the home she'd been seeking. She looked into the flames and closed her eyes.

Suddenly wolfsong filled the night. Howling voices echoed from below.

Kono leaped to her feet, her head held low, listening intently. The undulating song swelled from all around as distant wolves howled along and stopped, and others joined in, their voices rising and falling.

The hair on the back of Malu's neck prickled. The song of these wolves was a song of doom. She would lose Kono.

Trancelike, lifting one paw at a time, her wolf padded slowly to the entrance, looking out into the night. She stood still, head cocked, her tail held straight out behind her.

Malu watched in fear. Were the wolves calling Kono away? Would Kono go off to live with her own kind?

She wanted to call, *Come back, Kono!* But she didn't. She couldn't hold Kono, either with a strap or with a command. Kono would choose.

Kono pointed her nose skyward. *Ooooooooooh!*—a muted howl. Malu held her breath.

The song of the other wolves instantly stopped. Then one wolf howled back. Were Kono and the stranger talking to each other? Did Kono's howl mean *Here I am*, and the other, *Come with us?*

Malu bit her lips. The words *Don't leave me, Kono. Don't go*, tumbled through her mind.

Kono stepped forward, half out of the cave. She lowered her tail and stood like an image made of stone. After moments of silence, the strange wolf pack howled loud, once, and were silent.

Kono waited, turned around, and gazed at Malu. Then her wolf padded back to her, nosing her chin.

"Oh!" breathed Malu, reaching out to Kono with both hands, hugging her. Kono lay down beside her as Malu murmured, "Kono, Kono, my wolf."

* * *

The fire was still glowing when Malu opened her eyes. Kono was lying beside her, head on paws, looking at her. Remembering last night, Malu pressed her cheek against the wolf's long nose.

The air drifting into the cave was cold and damp. Kono went to the entrance, sniffing deep, looking from side to side. Malu, standing beside her, saw a mist hiding the far side of the gorge.

"Come, Kono. Let's get more mice, and then do some real hunting." They ran down to the stream and drank from it. Malu sat on the bank, warming her wet hands inside her shirt as she watched Kono catch and eat mice. When she was through eating, she caught more for Malu. Again, Malu caught only a few.

She sat on a large flat rock and lined up the dead mice. Kono, sitting alongside, watched Malu cut and skin them. There was a rustling overhead and a loud croak. A raven perched on a tree branch, its shiny black eyes fixed on the mice.

"Your turn will come, raven," said Malu. She liked the bold black bird with its keen glances and knowing air. She scooped the carcasses into her meat sack and stepped off the rock, leaving the waste parts.

Kono remained, watching the raven flap down to the rock and cock its head at Kono. With a croak, it pecked and gulped down the mice remains.

It was strange that Kono let the raven eat them, instead of claiming them herself. But maybe not so strange—she remembered a story Sosho had told. In the Great Beginning time, a raven shared its meal with a starving wolf. Ever after, wolves became brothers and sisters to ravens, and some said that when a wolf died, it was reborn as a raven.

Kono and the raven had recognized each other. Malu stopped in the middle of the path. Maybe the spirit of Lone Wolf, Kono's mother, inhabited this raven. Animal spirits had the power to do such things.

In the cave, Malu slid the mice carcasses onto a green stick and set it over rocks of the hearth.

"Our cave!" Malu said, looking around. There was only one unknown, but it was a vital one: was there good hunting nearby? She couldn't live much longer on mouse meat. She had already lost much of the body fat she needed to survive.

The wolf pack was a good sign. Wolves wouldn't stay long where there was no game. She rubbed her hands together. Game, she hoped, that was bigger than hares and birds—and especially, bigger than mice.

The mice! Malu pulled them off the fire. They were black, but not burned up. She ate hungrily, eager to be off on the hunt, but slowed by those tiny bones. Finally she had spit them all out.

As Malu gathered her hunting gear, Kono dashed about. Down to the stream they went, and looked around. They walked upstream, where Malu had noticed a fallen tree that spanned the water. Kono burst into a leaping run.

Why was Kono so excited? Malu ran after her. The wolf was snuffling noisily around the fallen tree. She dashed across it, and ran wildly back and forth on the far side, nose to the ground.

A jumble of paw prints in the snow—that was why. The wolves last night had run around here, greeting each other. Rump marks, too, where some sat to howl. Then they'd crossed over and gone upstream—single file, the wolves' hunting formation. Kono ran off, following their scent. Malu had a twinge of fear.

"Come back, Kono!"

Kono stood still, whining and staring at her, as if pleading to follow the wolves.

"Come!" Malu called in her command voice. Kono hesitated, and ran back.

"What a good wolf you are!" Malu patted her. She *was* good. Her first scent of other wolves had to be tantalizing.

After crossing the stream, they headed east and walked up and down some steep hills. Suddenly Kono stopped short. She stood rigidly erect, her nose and ears pointed up the northern slope. She burred a growl so faint Malu barely heard it.

"What is it, Kono?" Malu squinted up the slope. She saw nothing and heard nothing.

Could it be a herd of bison or horses thundering along a distant trail? Strange! She pushed back her hood to hear better. Still nothing.

Now Kono's deeper growl and her stiff-legged attention meant she was on guard. She must be hearing something she'd never heard before, something extraordinary.

Moments slipped by, and still Kono stood without moving. Malu was mystified, but she couldn't wait any longer. She must hunt.

"Come on," Malu said, starting to walk east again.

Kono looked at Malu but stood rigidly in place.

"Come here!" Malu repeated in her command voice.

Instead of coming, Kono loped away toward the north. Malu watched her go, wondering what to do. Kono ran back to Malu, tugged with her teeth at Malu's winter shirt, and loped away again.

"No! This way, Kono!" Malu called.

Kono ran back to her. She tugged harder at Malu's shirt—loped away—stopped—looked back, clearly wanting Malu to follow *her*.

But why? Malu was curious. And she couldn't go on alone. She followed as Kono leaped ahead, stopping for Malu to catch up, and so they went, northward across the slope. Another big hill loomed in the distance.

Kono stopped again, and Malu with her, glad to rest. Kono stood as stiffly as before, ears twitching, staring intently.

"What do you hear, Kono?" Malu whispered. This was different from the eager excitement Kono had shown for the scent of the wolf pack—and different, too, from her warning growls about the boar. What *was* this? She put her hand on the spear-thrower and gripped her spear tighter.

Then she heard it, barely—a faint, faraway sound. Her whole body tingled. It was like elks' mating calls, but not like them. It was like—like a sound blown by a huge horn, far away. They walked faster, toward the sound.

The sounds became more distinct. Bellowing, but not like any bellow she'd ever heard an animal make. The hornlike noise ended on a shrill, high note. Kono walked on, and Malu followed, struck with wonderment. What animals made such sounds?

An answer nibbled at her mind, but she thought—impossible!

They ran and walked, crunching through snow, crossing a shallow creek. Up a hill, almost to the crest. Past a huge tree, half sheared off by lightning, and then—

The bellowing-shrilling sounds—loud!

Malu ran up to the crest with Kono. They looked down into a deep narrow gorge.

At first Malu saw only the stream below. She squinted at the opposite cliff. Two enormous boulders bulked against the morning sun.

One of them moved. She gasped. Animals! Bigger than any creature she'd ever seen. Long trunk nose swinging from its knobby head—long curved tusks— hulking shoulders—

Mammoths! Kono had found mammoths!

More mammoths loomed up behind. The lead mammoth raised its trunk. The roaring bellow, rising to the shrill squeal. Malu couldn't move.

The leader went ahead, stepping down a trail, a narrow, littered ledge between the sheer rock wall of the cliff, and the steep rockslide that stopped near the stream below.

The leader was the biggest. It walked slowly down, carefully placing one enormous foot at a time on the sloping ledge. The others followed, almost head to tail. The smaller ones were farther back in line.

Remembering Sosho's tale of his first mammoth hunt, Malu looked again at the leader. A broken tusk, a floppy ear—Tusker!

"Oh, Kono!" She clung to her. "You found *our* mammoths!"

Had the Animal Master answered her prayers? Malu could hardly wait to tell the clan.

Oh! She covered her face with her hands. She was no longer in the clan. She could never go back to tell them about the mammoths.

But she kept thinking how the hunting band and apprentices could carry home huge blocks of meat, again and again. When they needed more meat, they'd come back. Like the hunters Sosho told about, they could chase mammoths down the cliff to be slaughtered. The clan need never be hungry again.

Only it wouldn't happen. She looked again across the gorge. More mammoths! They lumbered up over the horizon and down the ledge. They set their massive feet on the rubble of stones, which shifted under their footsteps, clinking and clattering into the gorge.

Three mother mammoths came along, each followed by a young one. Two of the youngsters walked carefully like their mothers, but the third one was bumping into its mother, swinging its trunk at her as if trying to run ahead. The mother bellowed at it. The young one slowed down, but was soon pushing again.

Turning as much as she could on the narrow trail, the mother swung her trunk at her young one. It dodged. Its feet skidded on the stones. It stumbled, slid to the edge, and after tottering there a moment, toppled over.

Squealing and crying, it slid and bumped down to the boulders at the bottom. It rolled off a boulder and landed on the stream's stony bank, and there lay on its back, its trunk thrashing.

The mother mammoth looked over the edge, raising her trunk and bellowing. The youngster's trunk swayed slowly, stopped, and dropped limply across its chest.

The mammoths ahead of the mother made loud bellows that echoed against the narrow walls of the gorge. Tusker bellowed once and kept walking. The others became silent and followed her down to the stream.

The mother followed, too, and at the bottom went to her youngster. She touched her trunk to its body, feeling and sniffing it head to tail. She bellowed a long drawn-out cry.

The other mammoths were wading in the stream. Two of them stopped blowing water over themselves and went to the mother. They laid their trunks across her back. Then all three went to the stream, and the mother drank and blew water on herself.

This was sad. Malu sighed. Kono, leaning against her, looked up at the sky. Malu did, too, and saw a vulture soaring down, closing in with tighter circles as, ever alert to death, it reached out its claws to land on the dead mammoth.

Other vultures came flying over the gorge. The mammoths took no notice of them. When Tusker started back up the trail, they lined up to follow her.

As vultures landed on the fallen mammoth, scrambling to dig their heads into its vulnerable parts, Malu's sadness vanished. The mammoth was meat—the meat of winter that her people needed.

This one had fallen by itself before her eyes—surely a gift from the Animal Master. She must welcome the gift. Hurry! Take what she could. Other creatures would follow the vultures' sky path. Already a fox was running down into the gorge.

Leaping from rock to rock, Malu descended and crossed the stream. Kono was already there, her teeth slashing at the tough hide. Malu hacked at it with her ax, and slid in the knife to skin off a large piece of this precious hide. Then she cut deep into the flesh, carving out a block from the haunch.

A jackal slunk toward the carcass, but Kono ran at it, growling, and it retreated a short distance, watching to seize another chance.

"You can wait," Malu muttered. She cut off more chunks until she had all she could carry. As she opened her sack, a vulture hopped close, its head extended.

"That's mine!" It hissed at her, and she swung her knife at its ugly wrinkled neck. She filled the sack and lashed it to her back. Kono was sitting by the stream, lazily licking her chops.

They crossed over, climbed up the gorge, and headed for the cave. From the top of the cliff, Malu glanced back. The fox, the jackal, and other animals were shoving and snapping at each other, eating of the mammoth. But mostly it was the vultures, and by now the carcass looked like a mound of flapping wings.

Let them all eat. Her feast, and Kono's, would come later. Tonight, roast mammoth!

# CHAPTER ELEVEN

Malu slowed down. The cave was farther away from the gorge than she remembered. She was following the tracks they'd made in the morning—boot prints and paw prints together. Malu and Kono.

Malu sniffed. Kono, mammoths, clan. Go back to the clan to tell where the mammoths were, or stay here and save Kono from death.

If only she could think of a way to save Kono's life *and* go home! If she left Kono here and went back alone—but Kono would follow her. And here she was, Kono was walking beside her, running ahead, dashing back to greet her. Her wolf. *Nothing* must harm her, ever.

She wiped tears from her eyes to see where she was. There was the big tree, slashed down the middle by lightning. It looked like a man with one arm, pointing toward the mammoths.

Kono. Mammoths. Clan. The mammoth herd would

change the life of the clan. No more worry about hunger. No more worry about the unknown dangers facing the hunters in their long searches. She, Malu, could make the difference.

Following Kono, she went down the last slope. A snowflake landed on her nose. A few more lazily floated down as Malu and Kono crossed the stream and climbed up to the cave.

Malu built a fire. She put slices of meat on sticks to cook over the fire, and gave chunks of raw meat to Kono.

Waiting for her meat to cook, Malu went to the entrance and looked out. The only reason she'd left the clan and come here was to save Kono's life. They had finally found what she was looking for—this cave, the perfect cave for them to live in.

She almost wished she hadn't seen the mammoths.

Her meat was done. She stuffed a piece in her mouth and chewed—so good, with the warm juice running down her throat! She'd almost forgotten the taste of mammoth.

Malu pressed her palms together. She *must* do both: tell the clan *and* keep Kono alive.

But it was impossible! She'd think about it tomorrow. She wrapped the bearskin around the two of them and fell asleep.

\* \* \*

Malu awoke with a start. Suddenly she knew. She must have dreamed how to do it! She must go home *today*!

She looked out. Clouds veiled the rising sun—puffy white clouds: no snow. They could leave *now*.

The plan was simple. She and Kono would cross the river near home, and she'd hide Kono in the small cave she and Varda used to play in. Kono could stay there tied up overnight.

Then Malu would go home alone, see Mother and Father, and tell the clan about the mammoths. She'd say she left Kono behind—not mentioning where. The next day the hunters could go back with her to the mammoths' gorge.

To get Kono in the morning, she'd need help, and Ardap would keep her secret. He could leave ahead of the others, take Kono across the river, and wait until Malu and the hunters came along.

She went over the plan again. The hunters knew about the ritual killing decreed by the Moon Goddess, and they'd never risk offending the goddess by killing Kono themselves.

Malu would guide the hunters directly to the mammoths' gorge, but not to this cozy cave where she and Kono lived. How excited the hunters would be when they saw the mammoths! Then she and Kono would steal away and stay hidden here.

"It's a *good* plan!" Malu laughed and hugged Kono.

Kono cocked her head at Malu. Her pink tongue

hung out between her fangs, her black lips turned up at the corners, and her eyes glinted—Kono's wolf laugh.

Malu packed the mammoth meat in her sack and loaded herself with her belongings. Going home!

They'd go back the way they had come. By retracing her steps, day by day, she wouldn't have to search or double back, because she'd stay in shelters she already knew. From hunters' talk she'd learned at an early age never to wander without picturing the lay of the land and odd markers—like the slashed tree that looked like a man pointing.

So tonight they'd sleep in the hollow among the boulders and be one day closer to home!

As they left the cave, a few flakes of snow floated down lightly. Laughing, Malu stuck out her tongue to feel their sparkle. There were no dark clouds, and the breeze was gentle. Even with the load on her back, Malu felt like running.

Down the slopes she ran, and climbed them almost as fast. She was covering a lot of ground. Going home!

By midafternoon Malu was pleased with how far they'd come. A friendly breeze at her back had helped her walk faster. Soon she could start looking for the big split rock she'd noticed near the boulder field.

The breeze blew up in gusts, and soon the gusts became a steady cold wind. She shivered and hunched over. Looking at the sky behind her, she stopped short.

The clouds, now an ominous flinty gray, rolled fast across the sky.

She bit her lip. It was too late to turn back. She walked faster. Kono stayed at her side, and Malu reached out often to touch her as snow blew at her from all directions. Thicker and heavier, it beat at her, mean little flakes, like shards of ice.

The wind was her enemy now, sucking the breath out of her, pushing her one way and then another.

Up a hill, down a hill, and up again. At the top of one hill, she pushed back her hood to look for the split rock. She drew in a sharp breath. She could see nothing through the thick, whirling snow. Sky and earth were one, now—all whiteness.

"Kono! We're lost!" she cried out, clinging to the wolf's furry ruff.

Sosho's words came to Malu. "We shall endure," she said aloud, and walked ahead. Her foot skidded down the side of a rock.

Her ankle! Pain, like a knife! She hopped away from the rock. Tears froze on her eyelids. Was her ankle broken? That would mean the end of her. Leaning on the spear, she tried to put weight on her foot. She hissed with pain—but at least the ankle didn't crumple.

She stood still. Why had she been so foolish? If she'd returned to the cave earlier, she'd be sitting by a warm fire now. She choked back a sob.

"Kono, find us a shelter!"

Kono sniffed the air and walked ahead, Malu leaning hard on her spear, close behind, barely making out Kono's dark shape through the snow.

More rocks. Darker. She bumped into Kono, who had stopped. Then, as Kono stepped ahead, Malu sensed she was inside . . . something. She swept her hand about her. They were between some boulders, and overhead she felt pine needles. A big tree was sheltering them.

"Kono! You've saved us!" Malu whispered, sinking down and sliding her bundle off her back.

She was in too much pain to care if she ate. She and Kono hunched close together in the bearskin. She pressed her face into Kono's ruff and cried.

\* \* \*

The howling wind woke her. With dread, she looked out. Snow, still falling heavily, had been swept into great drifts.

Maybe this was the field of boulders she'd been heading for. But no, there'd been no trees there. She was still lost.

She stumbled out into a waist-high drift. Oh, the throbbing of her ankle! She could barely push through to a low spot to relieve herself. Kono floundered around in leaps. They hurried back to the shelter.

"We'll never get out of here!" Malu shouted. "Never!"

Kono, tail drooping, cringed. "I wasn't shouting at

you." Malu talked soothingly to Kono, and received a face-lick.

Those high snowdrifts! She couldn't find wood for a fire. Kono ate mouthfuls of snow. Malu copied her, and let it melt in her mouth. She lay down and pulled the bearskin around her.

Later, she tried standing on her ankle. It was less painful. That was the only hopeful thing. The snow kept falling. Malu ate raw meat—not too bad. But the day was endless. She was stuck here! For how long?

Before dark, going out for the last time, she could put her weight on her ankle, though it still hurt. Maybe she could walk tomorrow. Maybe not. She lay down with Kono in the bearskin.

It was still snowing lightly in the morning, and the sky was grimly dark. She dared not leave their safe shelter, even though the throbbing of her ankle was almost gone. They ate and slept and ate. They waited . . . looked at the gray sky . . . waited. It was the longest day of her life.

In late afternoon she saw a pink sunset. Tomorrow they'd be on their way again!

*   *   *

"Blue sky, Kono!" Malu fed Kono, and chewed on some raw meat as she packed up. With the rising sun to guide her, she could pick a direction to head for. But which direction?

In the snowstorm, she'd had no idea which way they were walking. They could have walked in circles. The boulder field could be ahead, behind, or anywhere from here. Her plan of retracing their way back was useless now.

One thing she knew for certain was that the sun and the mammoths were in the east.

She thought back to the day they'd fled. After crossing the river, they climbed the cliff, going north. Then they went north, but mostly east. During that time they crossed many small streams. And those streams—they had all flowed down to her right; that would be south.

That was all she needed to know. Going back, *toward* home, she'd head west until she found a stream. Follow the stream to the river. Follow it downstream—west, again—to home!

Jubilant, Malu set off toward the west. Her ankle was a dull ache, but she trudged on through the snow, looking for a stream. Walking and walking. Eating snow again. Would they ever find a stream?

Kono disappeared into a hollow, and Malu found her lapping at a tiny but fast-flowing spring. Fine! Spring to stream to river! She followed the spring water downhill.

Small streams merged, and she was following a wider, deeper stream. The land was free of rocks and boulders, and the midday sun warmed her and softened the snow.

When Kono stopped to catch mice, Malu watched,

164

glad to give her ankle a rest. How Kono pounced! How eagerly she caught a mouse and tossed it in the air, to catch and swallow the mouse head down.

"What fun you're having," Malu said. "It's not just for the food, is it?"

Again they walked on. Where was that river? They'd been walking so long. The day was ending, and the hillside was becoming rough again. The slabs of broken rock looked like river land. Her spirits lifted. But still no river. Keep going.

As the hill steepened, she looked up at a rocky outcropping and spied a cleft in the rock below it. This would be their shelter for tonight.

She made a fire and cooked meat. They ate, watching the flames and listening to the night sounds.

Malu heard an occasional rustling in the bushes. Several times Kono stood looking out, swiveling her ears toward sounds inaudible to Malu. Once she heard a faint roar, like a distant cave bear—too far away to matter. She lay down to sleep, contented with a warm meal, good water, a fire—and Kono beside her.

\* \* \*

Morning! She packed up and started off. "I know we'll reach the river today, Kono!" Malu said, climbing slowly down the hill. Her ankle felt good, but she couldn't leap over rocks yet. Kono kept running far ahead and dashing back.

Malu stopped. It wasn't her imagination—she was hearing a faint splash of rushing water. She climbed down farther—and saw it. The river!

It *looked* like her river—fast currents swirling around the rocks, the ice covering the still pools. The plain on the other side, with cliffs and hills beyond, looked right, too. But she must still be far from home, for she saw no familiar landmarks.

"Come along!" she called to Kono, who had leaped down the steep side of the riverbank. On the bank's flat top, Malu walked fast.

They were covering much ground, and it was only early afternoon. Home by daylight! A waterfall thundered ahead. She drew a deep, hopeful breath. Below, through the bare tree trunks, she saw water splashing and glittering in the sunlight. Her waterfall! As Kono leaped down the bank, Malu stood and closed her eyes.

Almost home! She sent up a prayer of thanks to the gods. She smiled as Kono turned back up and trotted toward her.

Suddenly Kono's hackles rose. Her eyes glared fiercely at something up the hill behind Malu. She burst into a furious run, skimming over the ground.

When Malu turned to look, a pumping fear filled her chest.

A hulking cave bear was running toward them, his paws scudding through the snow—huge jaws gaping—eyes fixed on Malu.

She ripped everything off her back, holding only

her spear and spear-thrower. She fitted them together and aimed—couldn't throw! Kono was between her and the bear.

"Kono!" she screamed.

Kono paused for the instant Malu needed. She lunged and threw hard. The spear struck the bear's shoulder—good! It sank in deep, and the bear roared. Malu smiled—

But the bear was running as fast as before, even with the spear in his shoulder, and the end of it bumping alongside. He sideswiped the spear against a tree, and it fell out. Blood flowed, but he seemed oblivious to it.

Kono leaped and clamped her jaws on the underside of his neck. She hung on, her rump dragging on the snow. As the bear slowed down, trying to shake off Kono, Malu dashed back for the spear.

Rising onto his hind legs, the cave bear gave Kono a mighty swat of his paw and sent her flying. He turned to watch Malu, now downhill from him again, and with a tremendous roar, dropped to all fours to give chase.

Glancing over her shoulder, she saw how fast he was gaining on her. The spear and thrower were useless. She flung them from her. She heard his great snorting breaths. She'd never get away from him. One swipe of his huge paw, and—

Her feet pounding down the hill. Do something! Think!

Those two big trees ahead! Down there, between them—the flint mine shaft.

Mine shaft invisible in the snow. That white mound—the shards tossed up by the diggers! On the other side of it, the mine shaft!

Scramble up the mound, roll down the other side, flatten herself down on the edge of the shaft.

Roars thundering in her ears. Like a boulder shooting over her—the cave bear—almost touching her. Falling down—down into the shaft.

Gone! Oh, the roaring! Shaking, she sat up and peered down the mine shaft. That massive head, the blazing eyes! She shrank back.

He was stretching up, scraping with his enormous claws, trying to scale the shaft. Seeing her, he scrabbled madly, mouth open wide, teeth gnashing.

But he couldn't reach the rim and couldn't get a foothold in the steep rock sides of the shaft.

Let him roar! He couldn't hurt them now.

Kono! Malu climbed over the mound. There she was, walking toward her on three legs, blood dripping from her chest. Malu gently hugged her, murmuring into her ear, "Kono, Kono. My wolf, my friend. We're safe now."

Kono's leg might be broken, but her chest wound was already clotting. Kono would be all right.

Now, on to the play cave. But slowly. Malu took a few steps. She felt breathless. Must lie down. Right

here in the snow with Kono. Just a short rest. Then
go on . . . cross the river . . . hide Kono . . . and. . . .

*   *   *

"Malu! It's Malu!"
A voice. Ardap's voice? Then men shouting. She
wanted to look up, but her head was too heavy.

*   *   *

Malu looked at the hunter at her side, holding her.
"Father?" Her head rolled against his shoulder.
"Malu, Malu, my daughter!"
Then she heard a whimper. "Father, Kono's hurt.
Don't let her die!"

*   *   *

Where was she?
"Malu." Warm hands smoothed her hair.
"Mother!" She pressed Mother's hand to her cheek.
"I'm in my sleeping shelf!"
Mother nodded, tears in her eyes. Malu cried, too.
"I thought—we'd never—see you again." Father's
voice cracked.
"Kono?" Malu asked. Her plan! She hadn't hidden
Kono. The clan had her wolf.

"Sosho has her," Mother said. "He'll make her well."

Not killing her? Malu's head fell back. So tired. There was something she wanted to ask, but . . .

* * *

"Mother!"

But Zarbo answered. "Malu, you're really here!"

Ardap was with him.

"You found mammoths!" Zarbo laughed. "You did it!"

"Kono did. She found them." Malu sat up. "Where's Kono?"

"Kono is here, Granddaughter." Sosho spoke from the entrance. He walked in with Kono and patted the wolf's head. Mother and Father, smiling, followed.

Thongs bound Kono's leg to a stick. Malu left the sleeping shelf to hug her Kono, but gently. "She was trying to save me from the cave bear. She saved me so many times. Sosho, do you mean that Kono is forgiven—she can stay here?"

"She can stay here, Malu, and I'm glad. The Animal Master came to me in a vision and said that Gunto did kill Old Wolf. He ruled that Gunto's wanton killing was a greater wrong than Kono's bite in defending you. And the Moon Goddess has withdrawn the penalty."

Malu looked down at Kono. The wolf was panting, mouth open, eyes glowing—her wolf smile again.

Though Kono might not understand all the words, she knew the feeling: They were free. They could *stay*.

With an arm around Kono, Malu gratefully looked up at Sosho.

He said, "Malu, am I to understand that *Kono* led you to the mammoths?"

"Yes! I couldn't hear them, but she did. She didn't know what animals were bellowing, and she had to see what they were. I was going one way, and she pulled at me until I went with her."

"Tell me all about it," said Sosho.

She told them about Kono tugging at her winter shirt, the mammoths walking down into the gorge, and the young mammoth falling to its death.

"And Sosho, I saw Tusker! She was leading them."

"Tusker! You—you and Kono—found *our* mammoths!"

Malu nodded. Then she remembered what she'd wanted to ask earlier. "How did you know about the mammoths before I told anyone?"

Ardap answered. "Your bundle—the piece of mammoth hide. The meat, too. Everything fell out of your bundle."

They asked questions. Malu talked and talked—even about eating mice, and her plan to hide Kono.

Sosho stood up. "I must go and talk to the hunters. When you come to the Clan Hall for the feast, Malu, bring Kono with you."

"Feast?" said Malu. But Sosho had already gone.

Zarbo grinned. "Your mammoth meat. Your bear meat, too! The bear that was going to eat you—you're going to eat him."

He and Father followed Sosho.

"Mother, I can't find my boots."

"Wait," said Mother, reaching under Malu's sleeping shelf and drawing out new boots. "While you were gone I made these, to bring you back home."

They were beautiful. Her feet slipped easily into the warm thick fur. "They feel good, Mother. Not dirty and stiff like my old ones."

"You traveled far in them, Malu." Mother hugged her, and left to help with the feast.

Sitting with Kono, she looked around, at the fire in the little hearth, at the rock where she used to tie up Kono, at the keeping shelf—and on it, her treasure sack. She really was home.

\*   \*   \*

"It's time, Malu. I'm taking you and Kono to the Clan Hall," said Father.

With Kono limping between them, they walked up the ledge to the Clan Hall. Hearing voices from inside, Malu hung back. So many people talking—what a strange sound! She was used to winds whistling, ravens croaking, wolves howling, mammoths bellowing.

As they walked inside, the voices stopped, and then

there were cries of "Malu! Kono!" Fidday and Talva came to her, Varda and others, laughing and crying. They petted Kono and hugged Malu. Zarbo, Ardap, and their parents stood nearby. Malu didn't see Gunto, but maybe he was in the back somewhere.

A rush of people crowded around, many touching Malu, patting Kono. They were smiling, not frowning. Pushing close, not shrinking back.

Sosho, at the hearth, raised high the burin, and the Hall was silent. He beckoned Malu and Kono to the hearth. With everyone's eyes on her, Malu looked down. Father joined the hunters standing near Sosho. Sosho spoke.

"Behold Malu, and Kono, her wolf. Malu wandered for many days and lived apart from the clan. She endured many perils and made a great discovery. Guided by her wolf, she found the mammoths—*our* mammoths! Yes. She saw Tusker."

He held up the piece of mammoth hide and pointed to the meat roasting at the big hearth. "Behold these tokens of Malu's Hunt of Passage."

Hunt of Passage! These were the words Sosho spoke for boys who were being initiated into the hunting band.

Sosho continued, "The Moon Goddess sent the wolf to Malu. Because this girl cared so well for the wolf, Kono grew to become the friend and helper to all of us."

Malu heard cheers of "Ho-la! Ho-la!" She looked

173

down at Kono, lying at her feet. Kono yawned and flopped her head on her paws.

Sosho clapped his hands. "The hunting band will go now to the Magic Chamber. Malu will go with us."

# CHAPTER TWELVE

The procession to the Magic Chamber was led by Sosho, with the two image-makers, Ullas and Zarbo, followed by the initiated hunters. At the rear walked Malu, by herself, feeling very small.

But *she* was going to the Magic Chamber. To be a hunter, she must look a hunter. Like them, she walked with head held high.

The hunters with their torches turned into the passageway, past tunnels that branched off, small chambers and clefts in the craggy walls. The flickering torchlight made the hunters' shadows lurch above her like giants.

As they moved on, the light poked through the darkness ahead, but behind them the darkness kept chasing Malu, folding her in. She walked faster.

They were deep into the hill now. She shivered as her hand brushed against the cold wet wall of the passage. The hunters stopped, and she peered around them to see why—a barrier of rocks. Younger hunters, rushing forward, rolled them aside. Then for a long time they walked along on a rocky floor that tilted steadily downward.

Another stop—again, young hunters rushing forward. This time, they lifted a long ladder out of a crevice in the wall and slid the end of it down somewhere. Down where? she wondered.

And then, strangely, the hunters slid out of their fur boots and left them standing at the side. She did as they did. They climbed down the ladder until she stood alone at the top. She tingled with fear. Already the hunters and their torches were walking on, leaving her in darkness.

She quickly backed down the ladder, gripping the sides tight, her toes reaching for each rung. The rungs were smooth and warm, polished by the feet of many hunters of the past. Her fear vanished. She was following in the footsteps of the Ancients.

As she stepped off the last rung, her foot touched something soft and wet that oozed up through her toes. *Hoo!* But it was only sand and water. The torchlight was moving farther ahead, and she ran to catch up.

The procession stopped beside an animal hide hanging on the wall. Sosho's voice broke the silence. "Come forward, Malu. You will behold things meant only for the eyes of the hunting band. Swear to the Animal Master never to speak of what you'll see in the Magic Chamber."

Malu repeated, "I swear to the Animal Master never to speak of what I'll see in the Magic Chamber." She wished her voice didn't sound shaky.

Sosho entered the darkness. "Follow him," Zarbo whispered. She walked in, and after her, Zarbo and Ullas. She saw nothing until the hunters with torches entered.

She looked upward. There seemed to be no ceiling—the walls went up and up into the darkness. Imagine! So deep inside the earth, this lofty chamber, almost as big as the Clan Hall.

On the wall beside her a bison was galloping. Its gallop was so alive, its gaze over its shoulder so intent, that Malu's eyes followed where it looked, though behind it was only the bare wall.

An auroch with twisted horns was running. When Malu blinked her eyes, its legs moved. Or seemed to move. How could that be? Looking closer, she saw how its painted front legs were crooked around an angle of the wall.

She whispered, "I never dreamed anyone could make such pictures."

Beyond, two reindeer butted their heads together, their antlers entwined. Over there, a shaggy horse galloped. A boar pawed the ground, looking mean and angry, and for a fleeting moment, Malu could hear its enraged snorting and feel the dust kicked up by its hooves.

"What image-makers painted these?" Malu wondered aloud.

"Many of them by the Ancients. Ullas and Zarbo, too," Sosho said.

She followed him around a jutting rock. The torches lit up a picture, its paint new and bright.

She gasped. Mammoths walking down a cliff. Their knobby heads and humped shoulders, like real mammoths. Stepping down the path, raising their big feet. The leading mammoth, broken tusk and floppy ear—Tusker! At the end, with its mother—a small mammoth!

"The gorge—the mammoths—just what I saw!" she cried out.

Looking closer, she saw some small sticklike figures—hunters waving their spears, chasing the mammoths. That was the only difference.

Next to this, another bright painting. Her breath whistled out of her. This! A mammoth on its back, its trunk limp across the belly.

"Sosho! The *baby* mammoth I saw was lying there like that, too!" The painted mammoth was full-grown, and bristling with the spears of the hunters, who were dancing around it with their arms flung high.

"Zarbo painted these while you were away," said Sosho.

Malu turned and looked at Zarbo. He stood tall, hardly leaning on his stick.

"How did Zarbo know what I saw?"

"He did not know what you saw. Zarbo's forceful spirit makes strong hunting images. *He* showed the Animal Master our great need," Sosho said, "and *you* went there and made it happen."

That's what the images were all about! And why Sosho had pleaded with Zarbo, and why Zarbo, with the death wish, could not refuse to become the image-maker.

For a long time she gazed at the paintings, fixing them in her mind, and no one urged her to move. Finally she looked at Sosho, and he led her into another chamber.

On the wall here were no animal pictures. Only hands! Red circles of paint around hand shapes that had been left unpainted. Hands all around—so many hands! All different. Some of them had finger stubs or missing fingers. The paint around some handprints was old and dark; around others, bright fresh red.

The secret of the red hand! At last she knew. Each new hunter left his handprint here.

One of the brighter handprints had the same two fingers missing as Gunto had. Had they made a new handprint of Gunto, to reflect his dishonor? She couldn't ask.

"Over there is your father's handprint." Sosho was pointing to one of the darker red circles.

Father had held his hand here when he was not much older than Malu. She set her hand into the print. She looked around for Father and saw his eyes warm upon her.

"These are the hands of our hunters, from the time of the Ancients to our own," said Sosho, "and yours will join them, Malu. Place your left hand here."

She set her hand at the spot he was touching. Her hand was trembling, so she pressed her palm hard against the wall.

Zarbo was at her side with a clay bowl and a bent reed with tiny holes at the bend. Holding down the small end of the reed in the paint, he aimed the bent corner of the reed at Malu's hand and blew through the other end. Red paint sprayed over her hand and the wall around it.

She carefully pulled her hand away. There was the clear outline of it on the wall. She stared at it, at her patch of wall.

Sosho nodded. "Look well at your handprint, Malu. This far you can go as a hunter, and no further. You will not be a member of the hunting band, for your destiny is to become a woman. But your handprint will be honored by all hunters—those here today, and all who come after us, long after we will have joined the Ancients."

He looked around the Magic Chamber. "We shall endure."

"We shall endure," they responded.

Malu took a final look at her handprint. She would never see it again—but it would be there.

She followed the other hunters out of the Magic Chamber. She felt the cool wetness of her hand and held it carefully before her as they walked through the passageways to the Clan Hall. She felt as if her red hand glowed in the dark.

\* \* \*

Malu and Kono stood beside Sosho in the center of the Clan Hall.

"Let us all hail Malu and her wolf," Sosho said.

"Hail Malu, the hunter! Hail Kono, her wolf!"

Their voices rang loud. They were hailing *her*! Hailing her *wolf*! Their faces—smiling! She gazed at the clan in wonderment. The hailing stopped, and the ceremony was over.

Kono looked curiously at the hunters in the half-circle facing them. Malu saw Father's face, looking proud. She looked for Gunto, but he was not there.

Many came to talk to Malu, old and young—Olik and Laris, Varda, Ullas, Lorvu and her little boy Jurak, who had always loved Kono—and many others. Leaning against the wall were Ardap and Zarbo. Zarbo caught Malu's eye and grinned.

Ardap came through the crowd. "You got your red hand ahead of me, Malu. I leave tomorrow on my Hunt of Passage."

Before Malu could reply, others were talking to her. Then the women announced that the meat was roasted. The feasting began.

Seeing Sosho standing alone for a moment, Malu went to him.

"Sosho, where is Gunto?" she asked.

"The morning you left, his fate was decided. Considering his past broken vows, and his lies, the hunters banished him from the clan."

Banished meant forever. At first she was shocked. But it was right. Vows meant promises to keep.

"Malu! Come and sit with us," Fidday called from the hearth. "Tell us what happened!"

As Malu nodded, Varda came to her side, and together they went to join them.

Fidday jumped up and down. "You have the red hand! You're really a hunter!"

"Only partly," said Malu. "Much was kept from me."

"Tell us about the red hand, anyway," Talva said.

"I—I can't tell."

"What are the pictures like? What else did you see?" asked another girl.

"The animal pictures are so real! That's all I can say. I vowed not to tell anything about the Magic Chamber."

"You sound like all the hunters—all taboos and secrets." Talva frowned. "You can't tell *anything?*"

Malu had been like Talva—the questioner. She knew how Talva felt. Now she had to be like the hunters—a keeper of mysteries. She looked into Talva's eyes. "I can't."

Talva looked away.

Fidday leaned forward. "Malu, what was it really like, living all alone, without the clan?"

How could she say what it was like? Fleeing, looking for shelters—so often hungry—knowing that at any moment a hungry animal might attack—no family, no clan.

"I want to tell you, but it was so—so different," she finally said.

Malu saw her friends' puzzled faces.

"It was hard, and I'm glad it's over and I'm back," she said. "But it was good, too."

The girls drifted away—disappointed, Malu could see. Only Varda remained.

"You always dared to try new things," Varda said. "I have some of that, too. You never lose it, really."

"I know," said Malu. "We did some good things together. I missed you when you became a woman."

They talked about their adventures, laughing about their search for the Magic Chamber.

"And now you know where it is," said Varda, "but I won't ask you to show me!"

Malu laughed. Varda understood. "Nothing seems the same since I've gone away and come back."

"Oh, Malu." Varda had a faraway look in her eyes. "I'm going to go away, and everything will be different for me, too. Kronu, of the Clan of the Bog, will be my husband. The shell trader was here, and he brought me a bear-tooth necklace from Kronu. We will marry in the summer."

It had to happen, of course. Varda was really happy. She wasn't pretending, Malu saw.

"That will be a great adventure," Malu said, touching her cheek to Varda's. "We'll always be friends."

Varda pressed her hand, patted Kono's head, and left.

Alone now, Malu thought about her Hunt of Passage. It *was* a passage—from being the girl she was to being someone else.

And it was even more. The Hunt of Passage was like passing through the life of the clan. The searchings, the wanderings, the hopes of finding something richer and fuller. She had glimpsed something of what the Ancients had endured, and how her people had become what they were now.

Kono sat beside her, nudging her with her nose. "And it was you, too," she said.

\*   \*   \*

"Let us have music," said Sosho.

Ardap put his bone flute to his mouth, and his clear high tones shimmered in the air. A hunter blew deep haunting notes through his goat's horn. Another swayed to the music, his fingers holding little bones, snapping them together—*click-clackety-click.*

The drummer entered the Hall, carrying the hipbone of a mammoth. He sat on a bench, cradling the bone between his knees, and struck it with a mallet wrapped in bear hide. The hollow booming filled the hall. To Malu it sounded like the voice of the mammoth that had given the clan its bones.

She sat with Mother and Father at the hearth, running her fingers through Kono's ruff, letting the music throb through her.

Suddenly wolf howls—close by, loud—echoed through the entrance. The musicians stopped playing. Up and down the wolfsong ranged, and then higher, ending in a drawn-out *ah-ooooo*.

Kono padded to the entrance and stood looking out. Malu walked slowly after her. The sky was black, the moon pale and round.

"Moon Goddess, here is the wolf I vowed to keep," Malu whispered. "She is my great friend. She has kept me alive. I am grateful you sent her to me and let me keep her."

She heard a chorus of distant howls. Then all the wolves, near and far, sang back and forth, and suddenly fell silent.

She walked back to the hearth, Kono at her side. Sosho's eyes followed her, and he beckoned to her.

The hunters were talking to him about the mammoths and going with Malu to the new feeding grounds. Malu listened eagerly. She would see the mammoths again, this time as part of a real mammoth hunt.

Sosho said to Malu, "Kono will heal soon. When she is able, you'll take her on a hunt. You can show the hunters her ways, how she moves, how to talk to her."

"Yes," said Bromer. "We and the wolf will grow accustomed to one another—we who did not understand wolf ways for so long."

Other hunters nodded.

They *wanted* Kono now. She was glad. But what a long time it had taken them to change.

There was further talk about the mammoths' new feeding grounds. Malu stretched out and rubbed Kono's chest. She listened to the hunters as their voices droned on and faded away.

When she opened her eyes, the fire was low, the Clan Hall almost dark. Many had left, and others had fallen asleep.

She sat up. Sosho was looking into the dying flames. He stared long—beyond them, into a no-place only he could see.

Then he turned from the hearth. "A vision has come to me. One night next winter, when the moon is round like this, when Kono is full grown and her season has come, the wolves will sing here again. Kono will follow where they call her. She will stay with them awhile, and come back to Malu. In her belly she will carry little wolves."

Malu's eyes opened wide. Yes!

"Little wolves like her will join us. We will care for